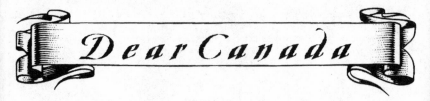

A Season for Miracles

Twelve Tales of Christmas

Scholastic Canada Ltd.

While the events described and some of the characters in this book
may be based on actual historical events and real people,
the characters are fictional people, created by the authors,
and their diaries are works of fiction.

National Library of Canada Cataloguing in Publication

A season for miracles : twelve tales of Christmas / Jan Andrews ... [et al.].

(Dear Canada)
ISBN 0-439-95270-0

1. Christmas stories, Canadian (English) 2. Children's stories, Canadian
(English) 3. Canadian fiction (English)—21st century. I. Andrews, Jan, 1942-
II. Series.

PS8323.C57S39 2006   jC813'.0108054   C2006-901085-4

6 5 4 3 2 1 Printed in Canada 06 07 08 09 10

The display type was set in BernhardMod BdIt BT.
The text was set in Goudy Old Style BT.

First printing June 2006

Table of Contents

Lo, the Perfect Plan by SARAH ELLIS......................1

The Keepsake Box by SHARON STEWART..........21

Stirring Up a Storm by JULIE LAWSON.................41

Small Beginnings by JAN ANDREWS.....................65

What a Blessing Is This Peace
    by MAXINE TROTTIER.....................................87

Shelter from the Cold by CAROL MATAS.........105

A Home Girl's Christmas by JEAN LITTLE.............127

An Unexpected Gift by GILLIAN CHAN................149

Dear Jane by JANET LUNN................................169

The Word for Home by KARLEEN BRADFORD....189

A Night to Rejoice
    by BARBARA HAWORTH-ATTARD................207

No Room for Christmas by KIT PEARSON...........229

Introduction

Sometimes a character speaks to me so strongly, by her actions or her words or her thoughts, that I just have to hold the book close for a moment. It's as if a friend has just told me something so true, so real, that I want to hug her.

I've had many of those moments while reading this collection of stories. A thread runs through them, one that reminds me of that feeing of expansiveness that would build and build as Christmas Day approached, a feeling that the extraordinary was possible — a season for miracles. It's here as "Silent Night" is being sung by one person . . . and mending a whole family. It's here in the moving attempts, often despite difficult circumstances, to give a special person a truly meaningful gift. It's here in the shivers of anticipation as Christmas approaches, in the scents of plum pudding and spruce boughs and cinnamon and cloves.

So cuddle up with this book in a favourite chair, and savour each story in *A Season for Miracles*. If you are already a Dear Canada fan, you will enjoy being able to reunite with some of your favourite characters "the Christmas after." If you aren't, you'll meet new friends who will write their way into your heart as they record their latest challenges and triumphs.

Happy Christmas, and Happy Reading,
Sandra Bogart Johnston, Editor, Dear Canada Series

Ivy Weatherall

A Prairie as Wide as the Sea

The Immigrant Diary of Ivy Weatherall
Milorie, Saskatchewan

May 1926 – April 1927

BY SARAH ELLIS

The homesteading life that Ivy and her family were promised when they emigrated from England to the Canadian West turns out to be a pipe dream. Some settlers gave up and headed back home to England; others stayed on, trying to scrape out a living.

Lo, the Perfect Plan

Thursday, December 1st, 1927

Dad has been reading aloud to us from *The Return of Sherlock Holmes*. Sherlock Holmes was a detective and he lived in London in the olden days. He solved crimes using the science of deduction. I have decided that I shall be a detective. Ivy Weatherall: the Sherlock Holmes of Saskatchewan.

First case: The Singular Affair of the Missing Raisins. Last Saturday when Mother went to make the Christmas cake, somebody had eaten the baking raisins. Who?

With the aid of this, my detective notebook, I am going to collect clues, and use the science of deduction to solve this mystery. The game is afoot! (That's what Sherlock Holmes says to his friend Watson when they head out on a case.)

Friday, December 2

It is all very well to say "The game is afoot" if you are Sherlock Holmes. All he and Watson have to do is grab their hats and walking sticks and off they go. Nobody says to them, "Have you dusted the bannisters, Sherlock?" or "There are pillowslips to be ironed, Watson." Mother says that running the hotel is a family business and we all have to lend a hand, but William's off working at the store, Dad's at the blacksmith shop and the twins are too little to be much use at anything — which leaves the helping hand of guess who? The Sherlock Holmes of Saskatchewan, except that what time do I have for the science of deduction? When do I have time to identify suspects by their footprints or their brand of tobacco?

It is especially important to pursue my detective career now, because today after school I came across a real mystery. (The missing raisins were more of a practice case. It was obviously Gladys. *I* didn't do it. Dad and William are too grown up. Harry only likes raisins after they are baked in a cake. Case closed. Except — when Gladys is so clearly the guilty party, how come I'm the one who has to interrupt homework, put on my boots and coat and trudge to the store for a pound of raisins? This is not deductive reasoning. This is whining.)

The real mystery is that after school today I saw Elizabeth huddled in a corner of the store, talking with Emily Piggott. What is going on? Elizabeth doesn't like Emily. Emily is silly. She treats us like children when she's only three years older than us, and we remember when she was sweet on Gerhard and told him that we were "nuisances." We have not forgotten or forgiven. Elizabeth will tell me what is going on, but until then this is a good mystery to think about.

Saturday, December 3

Elizabeth came over today. She didn't say anything about Emily. Usually she tells me everything. I had an awful thought. What if she is getting to *like* Emily? How *could* she?

I tried to stick to deductive logic. Sherlock Holmes doesn't get his feelings hurt. He just concentrates on thinking. Question number one: What is the link between Elizabeth and Emily? Elementary, my dear Watson. It is Gerhard. I asked about Gerhard, and Elizabeth told me that her father just gets angrier and angrier about Gerhard leaving home to become a musician instead of a farmer. First of all her father wouldn't read Gerhard's letters, and now he won't even let any of the family accept letters or write to Gerhard. I had the feeling that Elizabeth was going to tell me more when the twins roared in and interrupted. They are so bothersome.

Sunday, December 4

Here is something that is no mystery. Who is the most annoying girl in Milorie? Answer: Nyla Muir. Today was a big day at church. After the service was over we had the first meeting about the Christmas pageant. The Christmas pageant is Reverend Partridge's idea. Rev. Partridge moved to Milorie last spring. We share him with Manyberries and Vidora. I like him. He is very kind and pink. He loves baseball and in the summer he let the boys come to church in their baseball-playing clothes so that they could all start the game right after the service. Mrs. Muir disapproves.

Rev. Partridge explained that a pageant is the Christmas story done like a play. Today was the day for deciding the parts. The boss of the pageant is Nellie's mother, Mrs. McLaren. She said why don't we start with baby Jesus and this turned out to be a good idea because the decision was easy. Little Ivy Nygaard (my namesake) is the only baby in town. It doesn't matter that she isn't a boy because who will know once she's in swaddling clothes? Mrs. Nygaard gets to be Mary, because then if Ivy-Jesus fusses during the pageant she can settle her.

One by one the parts got decided. There was a bit of a laugh when Elizabeth said she wanted to be a wise man. But Rev. Partridge said that if we can have a girl Jesus we can have a girl wise man. I knew what I wanted to be. I wanted to be the angel. I'm not saying that I think I have an angelic personality. But I do have blond hair and I am very good at looking holy. I'm not bragging. This is just the plain truth. I have practised looking holy in the mirror and I'm good. By the time we got to the second wise man, however, I noticed that Nyla Muir wasn't volunteering for anything either. An awful thought hit me. Did she want to be the angel? What cheek! Nyla is already going to be the princess in the school play. Even Nyla Muir would not want to grab both good parts — angel and princess in the same year — I reasoned, using my powers of scientific deduction. But I was wrong. First mention of the angel and up goes Nyla's hand. I did not take this lying down. I shot up my hand too.

Rev. Partridge and Mrs. McLaren had a discussion. Then Nyla did a sneaky thing. She mentioned how much her mother was looking forward to making an angel costume, that she had some good ideas for making wings out of gauze and a golden halo out of an embroidery hoop. That was it. I knew I had lost. I knew that Mother would not have time, while running the hotel, to be making wings out of gauze. My nightgown and white crepe-paper wings was the most I could expect. Forget the halo.

Then Mrs. McLaren flabbergasted me. She said that she was relieved to know that Mrs. Muir was good at creating costumes. She (Mrs. McLaren) had some ideas about how to make an angel costume but she was defeated by the idea of a donkey costume and she would like to give the role of the donkey to Nyla and the job of donkey costume design to Mrs. Muir.

I did not dare to look at Elizabeth. We would not have been able to contain ourselves. Of course Nyla had to say yes or else she would have had to admit that the costume idea was a sneaky, get-to-be-the-angel trick.

I decided to be dignified in victory. My dignified-in-victory look is kind of like my holy look.

Wednesday, December 7

New guest in the hotel. Another travelling salesman. This one has something to do with tractors. More laundry and dishes. The Emily mystery is almost a week old and I have not progressed in my detections. Elizabeth hasn't said anything. She is friendly as always but also woolly-headed. Today Miss Hutchinson had to ask her three times to collect the spelling papers. Maybe the solution lies with Emily. Maybe I should find a way to go out to the Piggott farm in the dead of night and collect clues.

Wednesday, December 14

I've had the grippe. It is hard to be a detective or even a regular human being when you have the grippe. My cough still sounds like some animal barking. It doesn't hurt. It just sounds impressive. The twins were nice for a change. They came and did a puppet show in my doorway. I missed the Sunday afternoon practice for the pageant but Mrs. McLaren came round to tell me what I must do as the angel. I don't have to say anything. (Good thing — angels don't bark!) Dad says I look peaky, but I think peaky is a good look for an angel. I can go back to school tomorrow.

Thursday, December 15

Today at school my brain was full of cotton batting so I gave up on being a detective. I just asked Elizabeth about Emily. She said she was so happy that I had *asked* because keeping the secret was making her almost burst.

I was right. It is all about Gerhard. Gerhard has been writing to Elizabeth, but the letters have gone to

Emily, who passes them along. Gerhard made Elizabeth promise she wouldn't tell anyone, because he didn't want to get Emily into trouble. And Elizabeth did promise, but it made her feel like a bad friend to leave me out and like a bad daughter to disobey her father. And then she said how much she misses Gerhard and then she cried a little.

Then I confessed that I was jealous because I thought she was getting to like Emily and then Elizabeth said that she *was* getting to like Emily a little bit, and I didn't care at all because I am so sorry that Elizabeth's father is so stern and mean and if William went away I would miss him too. Then I cried a little bit.

The big news is that Gerhard is going to come home for Christmas, even though he knows his father doesn't want to see him. What will he do if Mr. Muller turns him away? Elizabeth and I talked about this all through lunch. Even in the afternoon the thoughts of it spilled into grammar. One week of the grippe and I seem to have forgotten grammar. Grammar does not stick.

Sunday, December 18

Last practice before the pageant. It was chaos. Mrs. McLaren had told the sheep that they could make soft sheep noises when they came up the aisle to gather at the manger. But they didn't pay any attention to the "soft" part and they were all baa-ing like crazy and drowning out the choir. Gladys and Harry were the worst. But I rose above it all, being an angel.

This was the first time we wore our costumes. Mine is my best nightgown. I have wings and a halo. I love the bouncy feeling my wings make. Elizabeth has a wool beard that is itchy, but she really likes wearing Mrs. McLaren's brocade dressing gown. And Nyla was right, her mother really is clever at costumes. The donkey is a wonder. The head is made out of papier-mâché with a wool mane. The body is made out of a brown blanket, and when Nyla gets down on her hands and knees you would really think it was a donkey. Nyla has sulked through all the practices. I told her what a great costume it was and she just looked at me as though I were a worm. Nobody seemed to be able to remember where they were supposed to be and Ralph (he's the first Wise Man) got the giggles and snorted through his nose when Hilda Hacker sang Lo How A Rose because she has one of those fat, wobbly voices. (I don't blame Ralph. I would have giggled myself except that I was being holy.) Finally Mrs. McLaren was starting to lose her temper and Rev. Partridge said that the first Christmas was probably very disorganized too and that we should all just pray for divine intervention.

Monday, December 19

Less than a week until Christmas! How can time creep so slowly? The tractor man is gone so Mother let me off after school and I went over to Elizabeth's to make Christmas presents. Last summer there was a paint and wallpaper salesman staying at the hotel and he gave me a whole book of wallpaper samples. They are beautiful. Elizabeth and I decided that we would use them to make picture frames for everybody. As we measured and cut and glued we talked about Gerhard. He will arrive home on Christmas Eve on the train. Elizabeth thinks that her father will not let him in the house and that will make her mother really sad.

I can tell that Elizabeth is worried because she is chewing her fingernails. We talked and talked about what we could do. Why is Mr. Muller so angry at Gerhard, I asked myself, using deductive reasoning. One thing is that Gerhard likes music but Mr. Muller doesn't think music is a proper job. The other thing is that Mr. M. is very German and old-fashioned and he thinks Gerhard is too modern and Canadian.

Then it hit me, like the shining star in the east that the shepherds saw. Lo, the perfect plan.

I know what we can do to soften Mr. Muller's heart. Elizabeth thinks it is a wonderful idea and she thought of one more bit to make it even better. The extra bit means that I have to be unselfish and it took me a minute to come around to it. But I'm willing to do it, because I have an angelic nature and also because that extra bit is going to completely knock the socks off Nyla Muir! The game is afoot!

Tuesday, December 20

We had the afternoon off school to get ready for the Christmas concert at school tonight. I'm reciting one verse of a poem called "That Little Christmas Tree." It is about what happens to the tree after it is thrown out into the yard after Christmas. My verse, which is now stuck in my brain forever, is:

What afterward befell it would take me long
  to tell:
It once became a fairy wood, where elves and
  dryads dwell;
And once a prancing, coal-black steed, With a
  noble knight astride;
And once a dark and gloomy cave Where bears
  and lions hide.

I try to make my voice dark and gloomy on the last line.

Reminder to myself: I need to borrow two pairs of

brown wool socks from William for the Christmas Eve plan.

Thursday, December 22

I have to have a diary gap. There is too much to say, do, remember, plan and make happen in the week before Christmas to write it as well. I will use point form, as Miss Hutchinson says we should when we are planning a composition.

1. At the Christmas concert I said "elves and dwayds dwell" but it didn't much matter because most people don't know what dryads are anyway.

2. I suspect, based on deductive reasoning and investigation, that I might be getting skates for Christmas! I'm trying not to hope too much.

3. Everything is organized for tomorrow night. Elizabeth and I are going to tell Nyla the good news tomorrow at school.

Sunday, December 25, just past midnight

It is Christmas but it isn't really Christmas until you go to sleep and wake up and I'm too full of what happened today — well, yesterday — to go to sleep.

The first step of the plan was to tell Nyla that I had decided that I didn't want to be the angel after all. I told her I was too scared to stand up in front of everybody in church and that I would rather be hidden in the donkey costume and would she please please switch with me because she had done such a good job as the princess that I knew she could do it. She was amazed and I think she suspected that something was afoot but of course she agreed. She was so grateful that she forgot to look stuck-up and for a moment I almost liked her, but then she said that of course she would wear her own store-bought white nightgown because it was much nicer than my homemade one so then I didn't have to feel bad about fooling her.

I thought I might be able to go meet the train yesterday, but Mother kept me busy preparing turkey stuffing and polishing the gravy boat. But Elizabeth came by and gave me the news. Gerhard arrived and Emily met him and they went out to the Piggott farm. Elizabeth told me that when she told Gerhard the plan he looked sad and then very happy and he said he would do it, which was a great relief because I sure didn't want to miss out on being an angel for nothing.

This is how it went. We all went to the church after supper, to the room where the choir gets together before they walk into church. It was a hubbub of costumes and choir members and shepherds' crooks. We put on our costumes and then Rev. Partridge told us we were all going to be wonderful and then he said a prayer and all the main people in the pageant went into the church. The animals stayed behind. We peeked out the door. All the people were there, but it was dark. Then the choir members lit candles and started singing. When they finished the first hymn it was the cue for all the animals to go outside, around the edge of the church and in the main door to walk up the centre aisle.

We went out into the cold but we were all cozy in our animal costumes. My heart was in my mouth when we got to the church door, but Gerhard was there. We did a quick costume transfer and he became the donkey. I remembered the socks for his hands and feet. The sheep were too surprised to say anything. Then on they went, into the church, baaing and hee-hawing, but not loudly, in a kind of holy way. Maybe somebody noticed that the donkey, crawling along on all fours, looked bigger than he had in the practice, but mostly everybody was looking for the sheep or cow that they knew.

I slipped into the back pew, next to Daft Binnie. He always sits there.

And then the story went on. Mary and Joseph and the baby. The manger. The shepherds and the wise men. The sheep and cow and donkey. The angel.

Ivy-Jesus made some gurgling sounds but she didn't cry. I never thought before how the first Christmas was like Christmas right now — there was family and travelling and gifts and music and surprises.

The final carol was "Silent Night."

The choir sang the first verse. Then just as they were singing the first "Sleep in heavenly peace," the donkey stood up and took off his head and joined in the singing.

Gerhard's voice rang out over the church. Without giving Mrs. Gilmour, who plays the organ, time to do a twiddly bit before the next verse, Gerhard started to sing in German. *"Stille Nacht, Heil'ge Nacht."* Mrs. Gilmour caught up and played very softly with him. The sound was so big and holy that I needed to hold on to something. I grabbed Daft Binnie's hand. He smiled his daft smile and held my hand back. Everybody stood up and finished the hymn together. I stood up on the pew to try to see Mr. Muller, but all I could glimpse was part of the back of his head and I couldn't tell if his heart was softened.

On Boxing Day, when I get to see Elizabeth, I will have to ask her what happened. There wasn't any time after the service, because everyone was in a hurry to herd all the sheep home to bed. But here is what I know I saw. I saw the Muller family, Gerhard included, piling into their car. And here is what I think I saw, in the darkness, through the snow dancing in the air. I think I saw Mr. Muller put his hand on Gerhard's shoulder. It might have been good tidings of great joy. It might have been a miracle.

Angélique Richard

Banished from Our Home
The Acadian Diary of Angélique Richard
Grand-Pré, Acadia
May 1755 – January 1756

BY SHARON STEWART

*Exiled from Nova Scotia, torn from family and friends,
Angélique and the rest of her family struggle to make
a new home for themselves at the House of the Acadians
in Baltimore . . . hoping one day to return
to their beloved Grand-Pré.*

The Keepsake Box

Le 1er décembre 1756

Maman always says that eavesdroppers never hear anything good. I suppose that is true. For what I overheard last night has left me worried. I truly did not mean to eavesdrop, though. It's just that we have to sleep close together with more than one family to a room in this House of the Acadians. People sigh and moan, and talk in their sleep. Some of them snore, too. Jehanne certainly does, deny it though she will. What I overheard last night, though, was Papa talking to Maman. At first I tried not to listen, but then I heard him say the word "afraid." After that, I could not help listening.

It's about tools, woodworking tools that Papa needs to make a living here in Baltimore. Papa has always done such fine carpentry. Before me on the table as I write is the keepsake box Papa made for my name day. He joined bits of scrap wood to make the box, then carved little pictures on it. Around the sides are mayflowers, like the ones in the spring woods in Acadia. And in the centre of the lid is a little farmhouse just like ours at Grand-Pré. You can even see a tiny wisp of carved smoke coming out of the chimney.

But more about the tools. Papa has none, nor any money to buy them. He told Maman he has just lost another good job for lack of them. At some joiners' shops they let him borrow tools, but at others they just give the work to someone else. The truth is that even with all of us trying to bring in a little money, Papa and Maman are having a hard time making ends meet. They also try to save a little for when we return to Acadia some day. Of course they do not discuss their troubles in front of us. But last night I overheard Papa say he was afraid we would end up in want. Yet he vowed he would starve before he would ask for charity from *les Anglais* who banished us from our home and shipped us here to Maryland.

Le 3 décembre 1756

It is odd how I cannot seem to lose this habit of scribbling. My beautiful diary book is full now, but whenever I come across a scrap of paper, I tuck it away. And when I feel excited or angry or worried, I write myself out. The paper I'm using today is wrapping paper. It is rough and bumpy and my pen scratches and makes blots. It is a nuisance, but much better than nothing.

My forefinger is red and swollen, and it itches. I must be getting a chilblain. And no wonder, for the weather is damp cold, and my hands are so often in water. But such is the life of a scullery maid, I suppose.

Le 5 décembre 1756

After Sunday mass, I went as usual to help prepare dinner at Master Hardcastle's. I was in the midst of chopping vegetables when I suddenly realized it is a year to the day since we first set foot in Maryland. It was the smell of turnips that did it. I cannot forget how we ate little else but turnip broth those last terrible days aboard the ship that brought us from Acadia. And the water so unfit to drink. Yet how terrified we were to go ashore, not knowing what we would face. We could only trust *le bon Dieu* to protect us. And we were right to trust Him. No matter how bad things sometimes seem now, we are far better off than we were on that ship. So I said a little prayer of thanks, even for turnips.

My chilblain is much better. Maman showed me how to make a paste of honey, egg and flour to dab on my finger.

Le 7 décembre 1756

Today on my way from Master Hardcastle's I met Claude and we walked home together. The matter of the tools has been much on my mind, so I asked him about it. He said it was true that Papa has lost many well-paying jobs because he has not the tools to do fine carpentry. Claude says the work he does in the shipyard is rough and heavy and fine tools do not matter there. But in cabinetry work, the kind our papa loves to do, and which pays better than any other kind, every craftsman needs his own tools.

Claude told me something else, too, and this has set me thinking. He says Papa has already seen the tools he needs. A master joiner named Abner Flint owns a fine set he cannot even use now. It seems his hands are all twisted with rheumatism, and he must leave the work to his apprentices or to hired craftsmen. Papa did some work for him, and said Master Flint's tools were the best he had ever seen. Claude says Papa's face lit up every time he set eyes on them. He asked Master Flint if he could buy them, but the price Master Flint set was too high.

Papa always thinks of our needs and never asks anything for himself. He has to have those tools. We must find a way!

Le 9 décembre 1756

Today I saw that big shaggy dog again — the one that reminds me of Griffon. I see him now and again and give him a pat. I keep a biscuit in my apron pocket, too, just in case. His coat is glossy and he has a fine leather collar, so he has a good home. I pray that Griffon does, too, with Jeremy back in Acadia. But I hope my dear dog has not quite forgotten me.

Dear Claude brought me a real treasure today. He got a job building a workbench for a bookbinder. He said there were scraps of paper — precious paper! — lying all around. He knows how I love to write, so he asked permission to take some. He came home with a whole sack full. I am rich indeed, for now I can write as much as I wish.

Le 10 décembre 1756

This evening I found the house in an uproar. Clouds of steam hung in the air and water droplets wept off the ice-cold panes of the windows. Maman and Madame Melanson, their hair hanging in strings, were stirring and stirring a cauldron of wash on the hearth. I was astonished, for they usually do all the washing they take in during the morning, hang it to dry, and iron in the afternoon. Then I got a look at *les Terreurs*. They are *blue!* At least, their hands and faces are.

It seems they tried to help with the wash this morning. Maman and Madame Melanson were out delivering laundry, and Jehanne was called to answer the door. The moment her back was turned, the twins got hold of the bottle of laundry bluing. They spilled it on themselves and dumped the rest into the wash. The best linens from some of Baltimore's finest homes came out bright blue! Everyone was in despair, for we could not possibly pay for the ruined wash if anyone complained. So Maman and Madame Melanson have been washing and re-washing the laundry all day, trying to get the bluing out.

Le 11 décembre 1756

Luckily most of the bluing *did* come out. Today there is only the faintest tinge, and we pray nobody will notice. *Les Terreurs* are not so lucky. Jehanne and I scrubbed them half raw, but the blue will not come off. I suppose it will wear off in time. I asked Marie-Josèphe whatever possessed them to play with the bluing. She said they wanted to "do the magic" for themselves — they had seen how putting bluing in the wash made the clothes come out sparkling white. Maman has given them a terrific scolding and they have promised never, ever, to touch the wash again.

But just in case, the bottle of bluing now sits on the highest shelf.

Le 13 décembre 1756

Yesterday we could laugh over the bluing, but today our hearts are heavy. Just one year ago our dear Belle died. Can it really be just a year since my sister passed away? The sorrow is so fresh still. Of course we grieve always for our other lost ones, too. We still hope for news of Catherine and Victor someday. But Mémère and Belle we will only meet again in heaven. At least Mémère had a long happy life before she died. But Belle was so young — why did she have to die? I keep the square of blue cloth I cut from the hem of her dress in my keepsake box now. The cloth feels rough when I rub it against my cheek. But it is exactly the same flax-flower blue as her eyes.

Alors — my tears have made a great blot on the paper.

Le 14 décembre 1756

I am determined that Papa shall have the tools he needs. Surely if I speak to Master Flint he will lend them to him. I wonder why Papa and Claude did not think of it — perhaps they were too proud to ask.

Well, I am not! The trouble is that I need to visit Master Flint. And how am I to do it? For I am supposed to go straight to my job at Master Hardcastle's every morning and return home the moment I am finished.

I must think on this.

Plus tard

Now I know what I must do. I have a half day off every week, and tomorrow is the day. I shall tell Maman that the cook *chez* Hardcastle has asked me to run an errand for her on the way home, so I will be a little late getting home. And I will use the time to go and see Master Flint. There is just one problem with this plan. I will be telling a lie.

Le 15 décembre 1756

Well, I did it. And perhaps *le bon Dieu* would not let my scheme prosper because I am a liar. Well, not quite a liar — it was closer to a fib. When I got to work I asked Cook if she would like me to run an errand on my way home, and she said she would. So what I had told Maman turned out to be only half a lie.

As soon as dinner was finished *chez* Hardcastle, I ran to the butcher's with the meat order as Cook had asked me. Then I walked down toward the harbour. I knew the way to Master Flint's workshop, for I had asked Claude where it was.

I found the shop easily, but at first I hung back, for it looks very grand. It has bow windows and the words *Abner Flint, Fine Cabinetry* in fancy gold letters over the door. But I screwed up my courage, took a deep breath and knocked. After a few moments, Master Flint himself opened the door — it had to be him, because he was so old. He is tall and stooped, with a grey fringe of whiskers around his face. He did not look best pleased to see me. Perhaps he was hoping for an important customer. But when I said I had come to speak to him he asked me to step in.

The shop smelled sweetly of fresh wood from the curly shavings that lay all around. There were beautiful pieces of finished furniture, too, like the ones I see *chez* Hardcastle. They were polished so finely I could see my face in them. Master Flint asked me who I was and what I wanted. So I told him that I was Michel Richard's daughter and that I wanted him to lend my father the tools he needs to do his fine cabinetry work. When I said that, Master Flint's eyebrows drew together so that his sharp grey eyes almost disappeared. He demanded to know why I thought he should do that.

I told him that Papa is a fine craftsman, but lacks

proper tools. Master Flint snorted and said that many a fool of a jobbing carpenter fancies himself a cabinet-maker. So from under my cloak I pulled out my keepsake box. I said that my papa was no fool and that this was his work. And that he could do even better if he had the right tools. Master Flint turned the box over in his hands, examining every join and carving. I saw that, as Claude had said, his fingers were all knobbly and twisted with rheumatism.

At last Master Flint shrugged and said the box was well enough, but nothing special!

My hand trembles as I write, just thinking about what happened next. I snatched my box out of Master Flint's hands, crying that it *was* special. And I told him he should be ashamed not to share his tools, when he could no longer use them himself. At that, his face turned red. He called me a saucy wench, and told me to get out.

I cried all the way home. And now I am very worried. I could tell from Master Flint's shop what an important man he is. What if he tells other craftsmen not to give work to Papa because I spoke so rashly? Maman has praised me much of late, saying how level-headed I have become. I am so proud of that. But what would she say if she knew what I have just done? I do try to control my tongue, but when I get excited things just pop out!

Le 18 décembre 1756

I have felt very gloomy since my visit to Master Flint. And what happened today does not make me any happier. This evening, Zachary was late for *souper*. He was supposed to have been working as a sweeper boy at the shipyard, but Claude said he had not seen him that afternoon. At last Zachary arrived and went to wash up at the basin. Maman went over with a ewer of hot water for him, and I saw her give a start and turn his face to the light. Then she marched him over to stand in front of Papa. For Zachary's lip was cut, and one eye was blackened and swollen!

Papa demanded to know what he had been up to. At first Zachary did not want to say, but at last the story came out. Another boy who works at the shipyard has been teasing him, calling him a "dirty Frenchy" and a coward too afraid to fight. So Zachary met him inside an old warehouse by the docks, and they fought. Maman was horrified, and Papa very grave. But Claude asked how the other boy had fared. Zachary said he was even worse off.

Papa lectured Zachary, saying violence proves nothing and he must never fight again. But underneath it all I could see that he was proud of Zachary for standing up for himself. I know I am! For, *moi*, I am fed up with *les Anglais*.

Le 20 décembre 1756

Zachary's black eye is now as purple as a spoiled plum. I thought his fight with the other boy would make things worse for him. But he says not. It seems the rest of the boys like him the better for it. So fighting is violent and bad. But also sometimes it is good. This is a puzzle.

And speaking of colour, *les Terreurs* are only pale blue now.

It is snowing again, big fluffy flakes. But even that does not cheer me up.

Le 24 décembre 1756

This is a month for anniversaries. A year ago today we moved into this house. What a wreck it was when we first saw it, and how hard we worked to fix it up! But it was worth it, for though it is crowded it is a real home now. And for that we all thank *le bon Dieu.* This year our chapel is consecrated, so Father Wentworth will say mass for us at midnight tonight. Of course we are fasting until then. It was hard today working in the kitchen *chez* Hardcastle, with so many good things being prepared for tomorrow's Christmas feast, for *les Anglais* give presents and celebrate on Christmas Day, not on New Year's Day as we do. But this year we are preparing a fine *réveillon* for after midnight mass, much better than what we had last year. I can hardly wait, I am so hungry!

I can admit here, though, that I am worried about going to mass tonight, for the lie I told hangs heavy on my conscience. Papa has not said anything about Master Flint being angry, so perhaps Master Flint did not tell Papa what I did. But it was wrong of me to lie, no matter how good my intentions were. And I am concealing the truth about what I did from my family. How can I welcome the Christ Child with all that on my conscience?

Plus tard

I could not bear my guilt any longer, so I slipped off to see Father Wentworth. He was very busy, as he has many duties on this holy night. But when I told him I needed to confess something, he listened. When he heard what I had done, he told me I was right to be worried. After all, I had lied to Maman, and acted deceitfully. But he said that God would forgive me if I truly repented. He gave me a penance of prayers to say.

Then I asked him if I had to tell what I had done. He said he left that to my conscience to decide. Will God forgive me if I do not tell? I have been thinking about it ever since, even when I was dusting and sweeping our chapel, getting ready for mass. The sweet smell of the wax candles made me feel a bit sick and dizzy. Perhaps it is the fasting. I

Le 25 décembre 1756

I broke off yesterday evening because the most astonishing thing happened. About eight o'clock there came a knock at the door. When Papa opened it, there stood Master Abner Flint! My heart sank down to my toes, for I thought he had come to complain of me after all. Papa invited him in, and then I saw that behind him was a boy carrying a big box, which he set down on the table.

Though I slipped behind Maman, Master Flint's sharp eyes sought me out as he shook the snow off his cloak. And he told Papa and Maman straight out that I was the reason for his visit. In two minutes, he had told them the whole story. Papa's eyebrows shot up, and he gave me a stern look, especially when Master Flint told him how I had spoken out and criticized him for not sharing the tools he could no longer use. When Papa translated all Master Flint's words for Maman, the look she gave me made me want to sink right through the floor.

But then Master Flint said that I was right! He said

that after his anger cooled, he thought about his dear granddaughter, who had died of a fever last year. She had always been fearless about speaking her mind, and he said I reminded him of her. Then he took the lid off the box and there lay his set of beautiful tools! Even I could see how special they were, and understand why Papa loved them so. The handles were of gleaming golden wood — maple wood, Master Flint said, the very best — and the ironwork was smooth and well-oiled.

Papa took up a tool and balanced it lovingly in his hand. Then slowly he put it down. He told Master Flint that he still could not pay the price asked for them. Master Flint rubbed his chin, frowning. He said he would not lend them as I had asked, because he did not approve of lending. I was so disappointed — I thought that nothing had changed after all. But then he said a wonderful thing. He said Papa could buy them over time — for a penny a week! Even we can afford a penny a week. So they shook hands on it.

I served Master Flint a cup of cider before he went. He winked at me and suddenly his eyes did not look hard at all. I looked down at his poor twisted hands and thought how sad he must feel to be unable to do the work he loved anymore. And how his granddaughter had died of fever just like Belle, and how he must miss her, especially at Christmastide. So I told him that my grandmother taught me how to make a wonderful ointment that helped rheumatism, and that I could bring him some if he liked. He said he would be "right glad" of it.

And so this Christmas Day, my heart brims with joy. Papa will be able to do his best work now, and will not have to spend his time doing rough labour for lack of proper tools. So I ended up doing good, even though I went about it the wrong way. I am still not quite sure what *le bon Dieu* thinks about that, but I trust in Him. May He always watch over us all.

Kate Cameron

A Ribbon of Shining Steel

The Railway Diary of Kate Cameron
Yale, British Columbia
August 1882 – August 1883

BY JULIE LAWSON

*Kate and her well-travelled family are stationed in
Yale, British Columbia, while her father works
as a supervisor on the Fraser Canyon section
of the Canadian Pacific Railway.*

Stirring Up a Storm

Saturday, November 24, 1883
9:00 p.m.

Today's headline: *Christmas Pudding Plummed!*

Plummed, not plummeted — although that might have been the case had I not had so many helpers — and I know "plummed" would never be used in a respectable newspaper since it is not a word in the first place. But at the moment I'm in a playful mood, and feeling very festive. Not only because the house *smells* like Christmas, but because it's been snowing all day!

This is my first entry in weeks, due to the burden of Chores and Responsibilities. The list is endless: helping Mama with the Christmas baking, cooking meals, cleaning, sweeping, washing the linens and looking after Mary so Mama can rest. Not to mention feeding Sheba and taking her for walks, going to school, doing homework and helping Mr. Hagan with the *Sentinel*

— although that's preparation for my future career, and certainly not a chore. Neither was making the plum pudding!

Toby even offered to help. He is good at mental arithmetic and Mama always doubles the recipe amounts, so that was Toby's job. We promised Mama we wouldn't disturb her, and we'd keep an eye on Mary, who was sleeping in her cradle by the range.

Promises made, we set to work. Setting out the ingredients was a chore in itself. Fortunately the hens are in a good laying mood — we needed sixteen eggs!

Next we had to weigh out the ingredients, cut the raisins, wash and dry the currants and mince the suet. Toby sliced the candied peel while I grated the bread into fine crumbs.

We were in the middle of cracking the eggs when Anne came by and offered to help. Good thing, because then we had to *beat* the eggs. Just as my arm was about to fall off, Rusty arrived! "Many hands make light work," Mama always says, and it's true. The hardest job was keeping our voices down!

Then came the debate over the brandy. Mama had put the bottle on the counter, but she hadn't left a wineglass. We needed "2 wineglassfuls" but what size? The choice was small or large, so we decided on large. Before I could stop him, Toby had added a *third* glass!

We had a grand time mixing the batter and stirring

in our Christmas wishes. I reminded everyone to stir from east to west because that is the way the three Wise Men were travelling when they first saw the star over Bethlehem.

By this time Mary was awake and demanding attention. I picked her up, placed her fingers on the spoon and, guiding her hand, let her stir in a wish. She must have been pleased because she stopped crying and didn't fuss when I put her back in the cradle.

I was about to press the pudding into the mould when Toby burst out, "Charms!" Thank goodness he remembered!

I ran off to the silverware drawer to fetch them, and we mixed them in with another round of wishes.

I kept my wish a secret, even though Rusty kept urging me to tell, and Anne almost ruined my life by saying, "It's written on her face, Rusty! See how she's blushing!" (I couldn't argue because it's true.)

After that, I pressed the pudding into the mould, tied it down with a cloth and set it on the range to boil for the next six hours.

A job well done! We rewarded ourselves by licking out the bowl.

Naturally the boys had "something to do" when it was time to wash and dry the dishes, but I cannot complain.

In the afternoon a letter arrived from Andrew, saying that he'll be leaving Victoria on December 22, and home on the 23rd. Hurray! By then it will have been four months since we've seen him!

Thursday, November 29

Heavy rains the last few days. The snow is disappearing from the mountains and the river is rising. If this keeps up, the stern-wheelers will have no problem running up and down the Fraser, and Grandma Forrest will not have to come by canoe!

What will she be like? I can't wait to meet her in person!

Saturday, December 1

Hell's Gate and Soggy Trifle! I could spit railway spikes, I'm that out of sorts, but is there anyone around to listen or care? NO!!!!!

Papa is miles up the Canyon, working on the bridge. Toby is off doing something with Rusty. Mama has time for no one but Mary, and Mary has been as out of sorts as her big sister. But Mary is allowed to scream!!!

The worst of my troubles? My beautiful gold ring with the sparkly red stone — the one Grandma Forrest sent me from England before Mary was born, so I wouldn't feel neglected with a new baby in the house — IT'S GONE!!

It was Anne who first noticed. We were practising flirtatious looks on Monday when she suddenly said, "Where's your ring? Did you lose it?"

OHH! It shames me no end that *she* should have noticed before I did. I've searched everywhere — at home, at school, in the yard, everywhere — and if that's not bad enough, Grandma Forrest will be here in two weeks and what will I tell her?

Great Godfrey! Has a part of my brain ceased to function, now that I'm worn out with Chores and Responsibilities? How could I have lost it?

My life is Wracked with Despair.

Thursday, December 6

Heavy rain, heavy fog, heavy heart.
At least Papa will be home tomorrow.

Friday, December 7

One week before Grandma Forrest arrives, and I am to Watch My Manners. My first lesson was this morning.

"You're a young lady now, Kate," says Mama. "No more slamming of doors and stomping your foot when you don't get your own way."

Have I been doing that?

"No more of your ill-mannered curses."

But "Hell's Gate" isn't a curse, it's a real place.

"No more of your talking back."

Being Mama, she says this in the nicest possible way, without a flutter of impatience or anger. If only I could be like her, a saint! Life would be so much easier.

"No more bursting into tears at the dinner table. Grandma will think you're suffering from hysterics."

Like last night? I couldn't help it! As for hysterics, why shouldn't I suffer, now that I'm burdened with the womanly chores of housekeeping, cooking and baby-minding? Worst of all: "I'd rather you didn't mention to Grandma that you want to be a newspaper reporter. It isn't seemly for a young woman."

Hell's Gate and Galoshes! Is there anything I *can* do to please Grandma Forrest? And where, oh *where* is my ring??

Saturday, December 8

Small Victory for Kate: Three Entries in a Row!

Put on galoshes and mackinaw and took Sheba for a vigorous walk along the railway tracks. And since no one besides Sheba could hear me, I gave full voice to my out-of-sorts temper and RAILED — mostly in the tunnels, and mostly over Mama's List of Manners. OHH! It felt good to behave in a hysterical, unlady-like manner for once.

By the time I got home I was a sorry sight, as drenched and muddy as Sheba, but it was worth the scolding.

Sunday, December 9

Papa left after Sunday dinner. He told me my ring would turn up as soon as I stopped looking for it. He meant well, but it did not cheer me up.

Tuesday, December 11

Mary is two months old today. Kate is two months short of sleep.

Thursday, December 13

A storm of activity has swept through our house. As soon as Toby and I got home from school, Mama put us to work preparing for Grandma Forrest's arrival. Out came the boxes of Christmas decorations, up went the garlands. Toby started putting up the cedar boughs we'd cut yesterday, while I arranged the nativity scene on the mantle.

After supper I helped Mama with *more* Christmas baking, then made some pomanders by sticking cloves into oranges. I hung three in my bedroom.

I was about to start my homework when a horse and wagon pulled up outside our house. Rusty! His mother is lending us a cot, since I'm going to let Grandma have my bed. Rusty set it up for me, and said my bedroom smelled just like Christmas.

He brought us some bad news. A big slide east of here wrecked a part of the railway line and blocked the wagon road with tons of rock. It happened this morning, and won't be cleared for another few days. So Papa won't be home tomorrow.

Mary was quiet as a lamb all evening.

Friday, December 14

In the space of an afternoon, Grandma Forrest has arrived, settled in and taken over. At least I have freedom from some of my chores and time to write in my diary. Mama had asked Toby and me to meet the boat, so the minute we heard the whistle we left school and ran down to the landing. Grandma Forrest was the only woman on the boat we *didn't* recognize, and she was the first to get off. She marched onto shore like a general — quite comical really, since she is short and rather dumpy — but the stern expression on her face dared anyone to get in her way.

No wonder Mama was worried about my manners! One look at my imperious grandmother and my knees started to shake.

She greeted us warmly, thank goodness. "Dear Kathleen! My dear Tobias! Just look at you!" she cried, then flung out her arms and crushed us against her enormous bosom. Toby was mortified.

I asked if she had enjoyed the trip. No, she said bluntly, she had *never* been so *cold*, so un*comfort*able or so *nauseous*. As for the *food* . . .

She grumbled all the way to our house, pausing only to ask us a question. But no sooner did we start to answer than she cut us short and launched onto another complaint.

By the time we got home we were exhausted, and eager to get back to school.

Saturday, December 15

Great Godfrey! Is there no end of complaints? I know Grandma Forrest has had a long and tiring trip, but why must she find fault with everything?

It was bad enough yesterday, the way she called Yale "a dismal little town" and Victoria "a quaint colonial capital." Not to mention the way she rearranged Mama's kitchen.

As for poor Sheba! Grandma Forrest doesn't care for dogs, so Sheba must stay outside at all times.

"Not on Christmas!" I protested.

"Bosh, dear girl!" Grandma Forrest snorted. "A dog doesn't give a toss about Christmas!"

And this morning! She told me that my bedroom is too small and draughty, the bed is too lumpy, and the scent of orange and cloves is "far too cloying." What's more, she lay awake all night, afraid that a spiked orange ball would fall from the ceiling and bash her in the head. So would I be a *dear* and remove them?

OHHH! Must go for a walk, get into a tunnel and RAIL!

At least Grandma hasn't asked about my ring.

Sunday, December 16

Church this morning, and of course the sermon was "too long" and "too incomprehensible." For the first time Grandma and I agreed on something.

She said the choir wasn't bad, considering we're in the wilderness.

Wednesday, December 19

Ever since Monday, Grandma has been firing questions at Toby and me "to prepare us" for the public examinations tomorrow. With me fumbling at mental arithmetic and Toby fumbling at everything else, she must have a low opinion of our intelligence. But for once, she has kept it to herself.

Mama joins us for our grilling sessions, once Mary is asleep. Sometimes, when she sees that a question has us stumped, she mouths the correct answer when Grandma isn't looking.

It's interesting to see how Mama reacts with *her* mother. I feel guilty saying this, but Grandma is not the most *agreeable* person to be around. She is bossy and opinionated — but Mama appears to enjoy it! "Go and have a rest, child!" orders Grandma. This, to my mother! And Mama obeys! While Grandma scrubs the floor, washes Mary's nappies and has supper on the table in the space of two hours!

She still hasn't mentioned my ring. Maybe she's forgotten she sent it.

Thursday, December 20

Public examination at school. I was more terrified than usual, with Grandma Forrest sitting there in judgment. We were able to answer the examiner's questions correctly, though Grandma thought they were too easy. "You need to be challenged!" she says.

I won a prize in reading, and almost keeled over

when Grandma said, "Well *done*, Kathleen!"

Tomorrow is our Christmas tea. Anne and I are helping with the decorations after school. Rusty is, too.

Friday, December 21

It's way past my bedtime but I don't feel tired. I feel exhilarated and happy to the core! Why? Because tonight —

No, I will not write it yet. All in good time! Though I pray Grandma will *not* wake up and disturb me. At least my bedroom lamp isn't smoking.

First of all, our Christmas tea was wonderful. An enormous tree stood in one corner, lit up with wax candles and Chinese lanterns. It looked like a forest in fairyland, the way the light shone against the dark green fir. And its boughs were laden with small gifts, each one with a name attached.

Rusty's parents had picked up Mama, Grandma and Mary and taken them to the school in their carriage. I was afraid Mary might wail during the program, but she was as good as gold. Some of our friends and neighbours hadn't seen her for a while, so there was a great deal of oohing and aahing.

After the tea was served, the program began. Our school choir was first, and in the middle of singing "Joy to the World" I saw Papa coming in! There were a few more carols, some recitations and then more singing.

Near the end of "Silent Night" an alarm clock went off. The ringing was so loud and unexpected that everyone in the choir jumped! Turns out that the clock was hidden in the Christmas tree and set for 9:00. No one knows who did it. One of the older boys, for a joke? Or Mr. Irwin, to ensure we got home at a reasonable hour? That would be just like our teacher, even though it wasn't a school night.

After the presents were handed out, we sang "God Save the Queen," then everyone wished each other a Merry Christmas and went home.

Now for the best part. Rusty had come into town on his horse and wagon, and offered to give me a ride home. When we got to my house, he leapt down from the seat and reached out a hand to help me. Such gallantry! I tried to land in a ladylike fashion, but lost my balance and stumbled. Then everything happened so fast — his arms out to catch me, my nose bumping against his chin, and quick as a whisper, a kiss! My first kiss!

Hysterical and delirious, that's how I feel, but in a deliciously good way. Will anyone notice? I cannot stop smiling!

Later

Grandma Forrest said she loved our Christmas tea. Except that the room was too hot and crowded, the tea lukewarm, the fruitcake stale, and the singing rather flat. NOT TRUE!

Why is it that when people get old they're allowed to say whatever they want, no matter how rude or hurtful?

Secret Thought: Maybe Mama had more than one good reason for marrying Papa and moving to Canada.

Another thing. Grandma said she'd like to give the Alarm Clock Culprit a piece of her mind. Spoiling a beautiful carol, perfectly sung (though flat) . . .

I won't tell her it was her own "dear Tobias." And I won't tell Toby that Rusty told me. It's our first secret. Apart from the kiss.

Saturday, December 22

The first day of Christmas holidays, and one day after my first kiss. I was planning to call on Anne — so much to tell her! — when Grandma Forrest announced, "Time for some air, Kathleen. You must give me a tour of the town."

What could I say? Remembering my manners (unlike some people), I graciously said I'd be delighted.

It didn't take long before she'd seen enough of the town. But she wasn't ready to go home. No, she had "a yearning to set off along the tracks, deep into the wilderness."

I tried to dissuade her. There could be bears, panthers and coyotes!

She gave a loud snort. "Piffle!" She said that any fool knows that bears go into hibernation, and "if we run across a panther or coyote you'll know what to do."

I warned her about the tunnels and trestle bridges, hoping she might be afraid of heights, or suffer from claustrophobia.

Her reply to that? She's "fit as a fiddle."

To prove it, she increased the pace. "Do you think I enjoy being cooped up indoors? I've been longing to get out. But your weather is frightful!"

The conversation then took an unexpected turn. "You must think me a relentless taskmaster, if not an ogre," she said — I could hardly disagree — "but old habits die hard."

She told me that she'd *had* to be tough, being married to a sea captain who was away for months at a time. She'd had to be *stern*, raising five sons and three daughters on her own. She'd expected — no, demanded — the utmost from her children.

"You and Tobias must take me as you *find* me," she said. "but that doesn't mean you're to *accept* everything I say. Not without a *challenge!*"

By then I was getting quite stirred up, and ready to take her on, but she wasn't finished. She said she was longing for a good debate, some intellectual stimulation. "If you *disagree* with what I say — and I know you do — *argue* with me! You know this colony better than I do — stand up for it! *Stand up* for your dripping wet wilderness and your backwater town! If you'd rather not do that, then you can ignore me as a tedious old grouch."

So I took her at her word. I put up an exceedingly fine argument for Yale, and for our railway, and for Canada. I forgot Mama's advice and told her about my work at the newspaper office, and how I wanted to grow up to be a reporter. I also told her that I liked having the spiked oranges in my bedroom, and had a good mind to hang them back up.

She wasn't the least bit afraid in the tunnel. When we reached the middle, we yelled "Merry Christmas" at the top of our lungs. I can still hear the echo.

LESSON LEARNED: Never judge a person until you hear their side of the story.

Sunday, December 23

Andrew is home! Half the town was at the landing to greet friends and relatives getting off the boat, and it took a while before he could reach us.

"You're the spitting image of your Grandfather Forrest!" Grandma said, and almost knocked him over with her bone-crushing hug.

I'd meant to warn him, but never had the chance.

Monday, December 24

10:00 p.m. and not a creature is stirring. Except for me.

I've let Sheba inside, secretly, and she's sleeping by the kitchen stove, worn out, like everyone else, by all the Christmas excitement.

It's wonderful to have Andrew home. We heard all about his time in Victoria and asked hundreds of questions, even about things we already knew from his letters, just to listen to him talk. For once, Grandma Forrest couldn't get a word in edgewise!

After lunch we tramped up the hill to cut down our Christmas tree. Mama stayed behind with Mary, but Grandma insisted on coming — and managed to keep up! Even though the trail was "too steep" and the wind "too cold for a civilized being."

"*This* isn't cold!" I argued. "And it's only a breeze!" That set us off on a debate over the meaning of wind, and the real definition of cold, with Papa and the boys joining in.

We'd taken two sleds up the hill, one for the tree, and the other for Grandma. Toby and I rode down with her, Toby steering and Grandma sitting between us. She screamed the whole way — but *loved* it!

Or so she claimed. She may have been too cold and breathless to say anything more.

After we came home we decorated the tree and put up some fresh cedar boughs and holly.

Andrew hung a bit of mistletoe he'd brought back from Victoria, and Mama and Papa were the first to try it out.

Tuesday, December 25

What a houseful of merry-makers and jolly Christmas spirits! Not only was our family gathered round the dining room table, but the Schroeders as well — Rusty, Clara and their parents. They even brought Callie to be company for Sheba, although the dogs had to stay outside.

The highlight of Christmas dinner was the plum pudding, and Mama let ME do the finishing touches. I plunged it into boiling water as soon as we came home from church, so it would stay hot. Then, when the time came, I turned it out of the mould, placed a sprig of holly in the middle, and poured brandy around it. Toby got to light it, but I had the honour of carrying it to the table — a gorgeous pudding, encircled in flame.

I was so proud. My face was burning from the compliments, and not just from the excitement of having Rusty sitting across from me.

Then came the test. Mama served the pudding and gave her usual warning about not biting on a charm, while I passed round the hard sauce. My heart was thumping with nervousness as I watched everyone take their first taste. What if I'd mixed up salt for sugar? It wouldn't have been the first time.

But it was grand! "The best plum pudding I've ever tasted!" Mama said, and I was regaled with another round of compliments, even from Grandma Forrest.

What with the fire in the grate and the number of burning candles — as well as all the attention setting me aflame — I was about to excuse myself and splash water on my face when Grandma gave an alarming cough.

"Goodness me! That was close!" She held up the charm she had almost swallowed and, with a boisterous laugh, said, "There's an obituary for your newspaper, Kathleen: She led a *charmed life*."

Groans and laughter followed.

Then Toby burst out, "It's Kate's ring!"

Grandma wiped it with her napkin and took a closer look. "So it is!" she said. "However did it end up in the pudding?"

I was too relieved to care.

Now I'm thinking that *Toby* might have done it on purpose. He was paying very close attention as people were eating their pudding . . . and he could easily have dropped it into the batter when I wasn't looking. I *know* I'd taken it off, as I always do when working in the kitchen.

I won't confront him though. Because then I'd have to *kill* the fiend!

Besides, I'm not angry. The ring is back on my finger, I found the good luck horseshoe in my pudding, and Rusty gave me a Christmas kiss. Secretly, under the mistletoe.

Thursday, January 3, 1884

Saw Andrew off this afternoon. There is so much ice moving down the river, the steamboats have stopped running. So he had to go in Captain Bristol's canoe, along with the mail and two other passengers. What an Adventure!

Now Grandma's moving her things into Andrew's bedroom so I can have my room back. HURRAY!!!

Can't wait to go back to school on Monday.

Monday, January 7

The nicest thing happened after school today. Grandma was upstairs rocking Mary to sleep, and Mama was alone in the kitchen. We sat down over a cup of tea and talked, just the two of us. It felt like old times.

"Things will get better," she said. "I know how you feel — the chores and all — but I couldn't have managed without you." She told me I'd have much more time to myself with Grandma here, and by the time Grandma left in the spring, Mama would have regained her energy.

We talked straight through until suppertime, about mothers and daughters and everything.

I hadn't realized how much I've missed Mama since Mary was born. Even though she hasn't been away.

And tomorrow, now that the weather has cleared, Rusty is taking me sleighing!!! This is starting out to be a Very Good Year.

Sophie Loveridge

Winter of Peril

The Newfoundland Diary of Sophie Loveridge
Mairie's Cove, New-Found-Land

March 1721 – June 1722

BY JAN ANDREWS

Having lived through a brutal winter on the eastern shore of Newfoundland, Sophie has moved to a community farther south, several days sail from the tiny fishing outpost of Mairie's Cove.

Small Beginnings

Tuesday, December 25, 1722

*Christmas Day. In Trinity, Newfoundland —
where I did not expect to be.*

After lunch

I have had A BRILLIANT IDEA. It came to me as I was picking up my pen to write in this book which Uncle Thaddeus made sure I would get as a Christmas present. All set in a pretty cloth bag.

Uncle Thaddeus sent the book on the last sack ship, with other things for us. I knew about those but I did not know about this. Mama and Papa saved it without telling me AND they remembered to give it to me after all the months had passed.

The IDEA is that I will teach Tamsin to read and write to thank her for helping me with the cooking and the water fetching and the fire tending and all the other tasks that I would otherwise have to do by myself so that Mama and Papa and I might live here.

I showed her my book as we were waiting for the Christmas prayer service — which was held at Mr. John Downs's store. Mr. Downs the Younger read the prayers because even here — where there are at least twenty families who are settled and who stay through the winter — there is still no vicar and no church.

Tamsin admired the cloth bag very much. She also admired the book's cover. Then she looked inside. As soon as she saw the inscription Uncle Thaddeus had made for me she shut the book up tight.

I knew she could not read or write. But I had not thought about it upsetting her. I hope that teaching her will be a VERY GOOD GIFT.

Yesterday we went together and collected pine boughs. We got them from the trees along the track which is there to get from one cove to the other. Because Trinity is made of two coves whereas Mairie's Cove had only one.

Tamsin's big brother, Abel, cut the boughs down for us. Once we had brought them in Papa tried to help us arrange them. Unfortunately, he made knots in the twine for hanging the boughs up. I think he will never be good at doing such useful things.

Mama, of course, was busy with her painting. She is always busy with her painting. When she is not out and about, walking everywhere all over, looking for new things to draw.

The pine boughs smell very Christmassy. I like their greenness. We put them mostly around the doors.

Tamsin is not here today. I have said that on Christmas Day she should be with her family and that is where she has stayed.

Probably I should put that in Trinity our home is really quite a lot more like a house. Although it is still made of logs. It has three rooms. Mama insisted upon it. Although she seems no longer to mind that we eat where I am cooking. And where I also sleep.

The logs are set side by side in the ground so they are upright. There are also logs for the floor which is much, much better than just having earth as we did in our fishing tilts at Mairie's Cove.

Evening

Mr. Downs the Younger had Mama and Papa and me come to Christmas dinner. Mr. and Mrs. Jenkins were there also. We ate roast goose, which was very good. Mr. Jenkins is to run the shipbuilding business that Mr. John Downs is planning. I should explain more about this. Mr. John Downs is the one who was Uncle Thaddeus's friend and who helped us when we first came here. He has returned to Poole, leaving Mr. Downs the Younger — who is his son — in charge of all.

Their store is not very big as yet. In fact, it is really just a room where there are supplies such as those who live here may need. There is also a fire to be warm and a space where people may gather. Papa spends most of his time there. He goes in the morning and comes home only to eat. That is because at the store he can play his fiddle without annoying Mama. People come also to listen. Mr. Downs the Younger says this is "good indeed for trade."

Trade is important. Even today there was much talk of how "ere long" Trinity will be a great centre and how the Downses's "premises" will play their part. Papa joined in most enthusiastically although Mama did not.

"Great things from small beginnings," Mr. Downs the Younger said.

Mr. Downs the Younger did not cook the dinner. That was done by his servant. Her name is Shauna and she is Irish. There are quite a number of servants in Trinity. When it comes to Tamsin, "servant" is a word that I would never use.

What a lot to tell! My fingers ache with writing so much after all this time. Perhaps I will stop. Only I do so want to say that I am thinking about Little Mairie and Thomas and the others from Mairie's Cove. Katherine and Peg especially.

I have said Christmas prayers for them already.

Before I sleep, I will say Christmas prayers for them again.

Wednesday, December 26, 1722

I am SHOCKED. Tamsin came to work with me again today. When I told her about my gift she was most excited. She said she would like to start learning as soon as she could.

I wished to ensure I would have all that is required for her instruction. I went to Mr. Downs the Younger to be certain he had stock of paper and quills and ink. He asked why I had need of such things. I told him my plan to give Tamsin lessons.

He looked at me most severely. He said such tools are not for the "lower orders." And anyway, those of the "common masses" — such as she is — cannot learn.

I reminded him — most politely — that Uncle Thaddeus had made an arrangement to make certain Mama and Papa and I might get what we needed. He replied that, since I am BUT A CHILD, it was for him to be certain Uncle Thaddeus's money be not spent "in frivolous pursuits."

I was so angry I had to leave VERY quickly.

Does he not know that Tamsin is the first friend who is a girl and who is of my own age that I have ever had IN MY WHOLE LIFE?

Thursday, December 27, 1722

I will not be VANQUISHED. If Mr. Downs the Younger will not give me paper, I will use the end of this book. Tamsin can start at the back and I will continue with my writing from the front. She can use MY ink and quills.

I had hoped she would be able to practise at home, but because Mr. Downs the Younger objects to my idea we must keep the lessons a secret.

Tamsin is another part of Uncle Thaddeus's arrangement. For coming here she is paid in supplies that Mr. Downs the Younger must give her. Tamsin has many brothers and sisters. The supplies matter a great deal.

Still she is very determined. (She is also very pretty. She has lovely black hair.)

Last night, the janneys came. Tamsin kept telling me that after Christmas they would. They might not have stopped at our house. That is because — although I do my best to keep to my vow that always I would treat everyone the same — in Trinity it is not so easy. People do not treat me the same. Some people are shy with me. I think also they are a little frightened of Mama. Anyway, as soon as I heard the janneys I opened the door. Papa joined in with the janneys' fiddler. Right there — in the darkness — the janneys danced.

There were ten of them, I think. They were all dressed up in disguise. The disguise is the whole point, so Tamsin says. I recognized Abel because around his head he had a shawl which Tamsin sometimes wears. There were others too that I thought I might know from the parts of their faces I could see.

I did not call out any guesses. The janneys must come in before you can do that. When the dancing was over, they all of them jumped and shouted. I am writing now quickly because it is after supper and I am listening for their sounds.

Friday, December 28, 1722

Tomorrow we will start the writing lessons. Today I concerned myself with drawing lines at the end of my book. I walked with Tamsin to her home too because I had need of being out. I talked to Tamsin's mother and held Tamsin's baby brother, who reminds me of Little Mairie the way he pulls my hair.

Perhaps I should explain that Tamsin's father is a fisherman. Not all of the men here are. Some of them are planters. The planters are people who own more than one fishing boat and have other people to work for them. Tamsin's father works for Mr. Philip Smith — I think Mr. Smith would call him a servant. The Smiths live closest to Mama and Papa and me.

Tamsin's parents are from around Poole. In that, they are as I am. Tamsin was born here. She says her father told her that for the men to go janneying house to house "be an old, old custom." I wonder why I never heard of janneys at Deer Park. Or perhaps I can guess.

Tamsin talks to me as we work together. That is how I know much of what is going on. Today as we were mixing bread dough, she told me that after Christmas the men will go into the woods. They will cut logs to be ready for repairing and remaking the flakes and stages for next fishing season. She says that of all the cutters, her father is the best.

Saturday, December 29, 1722

I had forgotten that learning to write is hard. Even for someone who is really clever, as Tamsin is. She did not get even get finished with A, which I had written at the top of the page for her to copy.

She pressed too hard. She made blots. She went home most discouraged. I did not tell her how Mistress Tyler used to rap my knuckles for such things.

We can write only at the end of the day when supper is cooking and there is nothing left that must be done. Tamsin is most insistent. I would like her to stay longer, but she cannot. She has too many chores to do at home.

Tamsin will need many pages. I see I must make my own writing shorter. I see that this book is far too small.

Sunday, December 30, 1722

We had Sunday prayers at Mr. John Downs's store as usual. This is for the people who are of the Church of England. The Irish people who are here and who are Papists, of course, must pray elsewhere.

When I saw Mr. Downs the Younger holding the prayer book, my anger against him made me want to rush and snatch it from his hands.

I thought of how my prayer book has been such a VERY GREAT comfort to me. I thought of how he would wish to ensure that Tamsin be prevented from learning to read as I do. I had to pray harder because I knew that God would not be pleased with me.

Monday, December 31, 1722

Tamsin did a perfect A. We were both so happy I made toast and molasses for us to eat. I often do make extra because I am not sure that Tamsin always has enough.

All day the boys have been piling wood up on the beach. Here too we will have a New Year's fire.

Tuesday, January 1, 1723

I will not wait three months until the legal New Year to change the year number. I have decided here in this new village, I will do it now.

I went to the fire with Mama and Papa. I thought of the fire we had last year in Mairie's Cove. Mama brought her sketchbook and Papa brought his fiddle.

The janneys were there, of course. Everyone was. Except Mr. Downs the Younger. He had said already he considered the fire "a pagan practice."

Tamsin has begun on *B*. I hope that will not take quite so much space.

Wednesday, January 2, 1723

I needed sugar. Tamsin would have gone to the store but I would not let her. I wanted to look at Mr. Downs the Younger and smile to myself with knowing that Tamsin can learn EXTREMELY WELL.

Thursday, January 3, 1723

Mama has made a very good drawing of one of the janney men in what looks like a wedding gown. Even Tamsin does not know to whom the gown belongs.

Friday, January 4, 1723

Mr. Downs the Younger came to visit. He asked Mama to make a portrait of him. He says his "beloved fiancée" in England misses him and would like to have something of him nearby.

His visit upset me. I know that I am right to be angry with him, but I know also how kind he can be. When we first arrived in Trinity he took me walking with him so I would know my way about.

Saturday, January 5, 1723

Tamsin remembered that if Mr. Downs is to come here to pose for his portrait she will have to call me Mistress Sophie in his presence. I said I would call her Mistress Tamsin. All day we curtseyed to each other and we both of us laughed. Laughing seemed the best thing to do, but the matter really is not funny. I do not think anyone should be curtseying to anyone. Except perhaps the King and Queen.

Tamsin insists the pine boughs must be put out before tomorrow midnight because it is Twelfth Night. If they are not, the year will be unlucky. I do not want to risk that. (Last year I forgot about Twelfth Night completely. But then we had no decorations at Mairie's Cove.)

Tamsin also told me she thought that Mrs. Jenkins does not want to be here. A girl goes to work for her. That girl's name is Jeannie. Jeannie says Mrs. Jenkins cries "a deal too much."

Sunday, January 6, 1723

Perhaps God has given me an answer. As I was praying, I knew I must stop being angry. If I wish to win Mr. Downs the Younger over, I must do something for him that he will like.

This is the last night for the janneys. Tamsin says it will be "the wildest time of all." She says she wishes she could go janneying — just once even — but girls are not allowed.

The pine boughs are not forgotten. I am going to take them from the house at once.

Monday, January 7, 1723

Tamsin has found a way to practise with pieces of charcoal from the fire. She makes her letters on the hearthstone first and then she rubs them out. Even with this, I think she will still need at least one whole page to get C right with quill and ink.

Mrs. Black came to visit. She is the wife of Mr. Jacob Black, who is a planter. I think Mrs. Black only comes to see what I am doing. I do not like her very much.

Tuesday, January 8, 1723

In my head, I made Mr. Downs the Younger a poem. I went to him and asked him for paper so I could write it out. He has not come yet to pose for his portrait. He says he must make sure his accounts are all in order. He truly does work VERY HARD.

Wednesday, January 9, 1723

My poem for Mr. Downs the Younger says:

Mr. Downs will one day be
Known o'er the world
And o'er the sea
For his great work in Trinity.

I told him he was the Mr. Downs that I had written of. He pinned the poem on the wall in the store. He spoke to Papa about it. He said he hoped he too might have a daughter such as I am in some future time.

I thought perhaps Papa might speak of his own poetry, but he did not do so. My poem is, of course, not so poetical as his was meant to be.

The name of Mr. Downs the Younger's fiancée is

Elizabeth. I asked him when she would come here. He said he is afraid she will find the clime "too rugged." Although he hopes that if he can get a house that is made of boards, instead of logs, it will help.

Thursday, January 10, 1723

Tamsin told me a hard thing. She said one of the reasons she wants to learn to read and write is so she may see what Mr. Downs the Younger puts in his ledgers. She wishes to do this because her father is always telling her they are being cheated. He says "that be the way of merchants and that always will."

I wanted to reprimand Tamsin as I have never done before. Although in the end I did not.

Could what she says be true? I do not think so. Uncle Thaddeus would not cheat. Of that, I am QUITE CERTAIN.

Here is the problem though. The catch for the season is often not enough. When it is not, people must get supplies "on credit." That means they are paying in what they hope they will gain, and not what they have. They are bound to the merchants by some means I do not quite understand.

Also here there is almost no money. It is like Uncle Thaddeus's "arrangements." One thing is for another, but no one gets anything to put in a pocket or a purse.

Perhaps it would be better if there was more than one merchant here. But there is not. Still, what if there were none at all? Do I not know of that? Have I not seen how terrible it is to try to manage when supplies run out?

Friday, January 11, 1723

I have started to read to Tamsin from my last year's journal. When I do so, I move my fingers beneath the words so she can see what they are. Also whenever it says "a" something I have her make the sound.

Tamsin says I am her very best friend IN ALL THE WORLD.

Saturday, January 12, 1723

A great storm has blown up. The house is shaking with the wind. I have put rags under the doors to stop the drafts. At least when a storm comes during winter there are no boats at sea for us to fear about.

Mama is making a portrait of Mr. Downs the Younger without him knowing about it. She is doing it from a sketch she made on Christmas Day.

Sunday, January 13, 1723

We gave thanks that the storm had done so little damage. The service was delayed, however. Because it took so long for everyone to dig tracks through the snow because the houses are so dotted all about.

As usual, Mr. Downs the Younger sent a boy to dig the snow for us. His name is Hal. He stacked our wood before the winter came. I think Hal is yet another of Uncle Thaddeus's "arrangements." His family lives very close to the water. Their home is much more like a tilt, as all the homes closest to the water are.

Now that Tamsin has discovered about the hearth-stone, I can call out the sounds of the letters for her to write them without copying. Already she is learning more quickly. Already she is up to *H*.

I want to make another poem for Mr. Downs the Younger, but I am finding it harder. I keep thinking of what Tamsin said. Then I remember Mr. Downs's concern for his fiancée, and how much I like the name Elizabeth. Perhaps it will be simpler to write about the store.

Monday, January 14, 1723

I wrote *Baa* for Tamsin on the hearthstone. She puzzled and puzzled and then she said it out. She read it over and over because she did not want to forget it. She was so pleased to have read a whole word that she cried.

We must AT LEAST get through to the end of the alphabet. I have divided the pages accordingly. Even with making half a page for each remaining letter, my own pages are almost run out.

Tuesday, January 15, 1723

Here is the second poem.

Should you be in need of a nail
Or perhaps a pail
Of line, or rope, or hooks
Of cloth or dish
Or salt for fish
Of knife or fork
Or salt for pork
Of needle for sewing
Or yeast for spruce beer brewing
Visit the Younger Mr. Downs
Where what you seek will soon be found.

The line about spruce beer is not right, but *brewing* is the only thing I could think of to almost rhyme with *sewing*. Also, spruce beer is important, so I left it in.

Wednesday, January 16, 1723

RELIEF AND VICTORY. I gave Mr. Downs the Younger my second poem also. I explained how there were others who might write poems for him if he would BUT ALLOW THEM THE CHANCE. I showed him what Tamsin has done. Even if I was trembling when I did it, for fear of what he might say to me. And for fear for Tamsin's family as well.

I do not know if the poems helped. I just know he smiled a little.

"What's done cannot be undone again, now can it?" he said to me.

I knew then that all was well. He explained to me though that paper is in short supply here. I am not to go to him for more until my book is "well used up."

Tamsin is very joyful. I asked her if she would tell her parents what she has been doing. She says most likely that she will.

Thursday, January 17, 1723

The secret is out. All need for it is finished. How lucky to have arrived at this conclusion when there is no more space for me to write.

Tamsin's parents are actually pleased with her. They believe she may have "chance for betterment." "Chance for betterment" seems to be what everyone wants in this New World.

Hélène St. Onge

Alone in an Untamed Land

The *Filles du Roi* Diary of Hélène St. Onge
Montréal, New France
May 1666 – May 1667

BY MAXINE TROTTIER

Hélène St. Onge began her voyage to New France with her sister, Catherine, who died on the voyage. She wed in the summer of 1667 and became not only a wife but a step-mother.

What a Blessing Is This Peace

Le 9 décembre 1667, *tard la nuit*

I do not need a candle by which to write, as the full moon on the snow that covers Montréal gives light enough. I should be content. New France is at peace with the Iroquois, my step-daughter Kateri and her dog Ourson sleep in her small room down the hall, our house is safe, our larder full, and Christmas will soon be upon us. With Minette and Sottise purring near Jean's feet and our bed piled with the quilts that Tante Barbe and I fashioned from goose feathers this fall past, I am warm and comfortable.

And so very unhappy, although I can tell no one of this.

Le 10 décembre 1667

A few moments in which to write before our day of work begins. While Jean labours in his gun shop, there will be bread to bake and linens to air. I must also walk over to the inn later and help Tante Barbe make a *potage* of salt cod and onions for any passers-by who may wish to take a meal there. Perhaps if I work hard I can forget what I heard yesterday. Why did I stand in silence in the kitchen, listening while Jean spoke to a customer? Why can I not control my curiosity? Papa used to say that eavesdropping behind doors may tell you things you have no wish to know.

He was correct.

Tard

How strange life is. One moment I am filled with misery and the next? *Joie!* Later, though. The common room is filled with men all calling for their dinners and cups of spruce beer.

Plus tard

If this is to be a faithful record of my life here in New France, it must be as clear as possible, yet I can see now that what I have written makes little sense.

So. Yesterday, a new friend of Jean's came into the gun shop. It was the Cavalier de la Salle, who arrived here from France only last month, a fellow who ceaselessly talks of exploring the wilderness. He wished to have Jean undertake a small repair on his musket. "When do you leave?" he asked my husband, saying that Jean was wise to journey to the Mohawk encampment without his wife and daughter, since the wilderness was no place for females.

Jean answered, but I could only hear the blood thundering in my ears. For the rest of the day I fought hard with my feelings. If Jean must visit the Mohawk and say nothing to me about it, who was I to interfere? Yet by the time we were at the inn supping with Tante Barbe, by the time the bowls were cleared away, Jean's pipe was lit and my knitting was in my hands, my temper was not good. As I have written before in my journal, I have a terrible temper.

Tante Barbe looked at my face, then at my knitting, and said that if my knitting became any tighter, Jean would not be able to wiggle his toes in the stocking.

How unfortunate, I thought. Perhaps it will keep him here at home.

When Kateri remarked that my cheeks were very red and wondered if I was becoming feverish, her father said, "I pray not. How can you travel with me if you are ill, Hélène?"

I? I was to travel with him? It seemed I was, for I must finally meet Kateri's grandparents and the rest of her maternal family. They are there at the new mission at La Prairie, having come out of curiosity and planning to remain only a short while. Kateri would come too, of course. It would be a mere stroll of only half a day's journey. Seraphim would remain here to watch Jean's shop during the time we would be gone. Tante Barbe would care for the cats and dog, preferring to remain by her own fire, *merci*. A short visit only, since Christmas was nearly upon us.

I met Jean's eyes then, and I could tell he had known the source of my irritation, and that curiosity — I am doomed to it — had again overcome my good manners. But he only laughed and said how surprised I must be.

Mon cher Jean. How well he has come to know me in these few months since we wed.

Le 11 décembre 1667

I helped Tante Barbe set out her new *crèche* this evening, one I fear she will have to guard closely. Minette and Sottise are already eyeing the small wax figures made by the nuns here in Montréal, ready to bat them with curious paws.

We are ready to depart in the morning. I must admit that packing of any sort is always *aigre-doux* and fills me with a mixture of sadness and happiness. How long ago it seems that I helped my sister Catherine pack once she made the decision to come to New France as a *fille à marier*. So many deaths, so much suffering, and yet what great happiness has come to be mine here in this untamed land.

Enough. I will wipe my quill and pack it and this diary. Our two *traînes* are loaded; the snowshoes stand near the door. By tomorrow, we will be among the Mohawk.

Le 14 décembre 1667

At the Mission

It has, as the date of my entry shows, been impossible to write these last few days. Only now have I been able to slip away from the feasting and celebrations. Jean has told me many stories of the Mohawk and other tribes, but nothing prepared me for this.

Le 15 décembre 1667

As the sun rose, Jean set out for a day of hunting with a few warriors. I will have work to do — it is impossible to escape household responsibilities, even here — but for now I am left to myself. Kateri is asleep next to me, wrapped in warm blankets, just the top of her head showing.

So. Our journey was no mere stroll, as walking on snowshoes through deep snow tires the legs. The forest was so beautiful and the calling of birds so cheerful, but even with the sun shining, the cold was bitter.

"Il est froid comme le marteau de Saint-Éloi," Jean observed in time. I would have thought Saint-Éloi's hammer would have been hot rather than cold — Saint Éloi being the patron saint of metalworkers and gunsmiths — but I was too cold myself to say so. I can recall thinking that I was glad of my wool mittens and the warm moccasins on my feet, and that Tante Barbe's own feet must be very comfortable if she was sitting by the fire . . . and then, there it was.

La Prairie, the mission founded just this fall by Père Raffeix, a priest from Montréal. A few warriors were just entering the palisade that surrounded it, but when they saw us a great shout went up and they came running on their snowshoes, muskets in their hands. Jean and Kateri called out and began to run as well. What a reunion it was, with all the back slapping and embracing and Mohawk greetings.

Jean looked well, they said, calling him by his Mohawk name, Sawatis. And Kateri — she was a woman grown! Then, "This is your wife?" they asked, crowding around me. "Her name makes no sense. She will have a Mohawk name in time."

Then the next words! Jean though, only laughed aloud and answered, "Children? We are wed but four months, my friends. All in good time, and take care what you say. My wife has enough Mohawk now to understand what you have asked."

How I blushed at that, but there was little time for it, since we were being taken to the palisade and led through a maze that Jean had told me was built for protection. Once inside I saw longhouses, just as I knew I would, but with them stood two *cabanes* built of plain boards.

I would have thought it proper to go to the priest's house — I could hear the sound of a hymn coming from it — and pay our respects, but it seemed it was not. Instead, we were taken to one of the smallest longhouses, where it was necessary to stoop to enter the low doorway. I could see a group of people seated around a fire. An old woman and an old man rose to their feet slowly, and held out their arms. In an instant Kateri was in their embrace. "Ákhsotha! Rakhsotha!" Kateri called through her tears, and I knew that they were her grandmother and grandfather.

"Sawatis!" called the old man to Jean. "Come to our fire, my son." Jean led me to them and we sat down together. As the old man studied me, the silence went on so long that I felt beads of sweat forming on my upper lip. He would be remembering his daughter, I thought. He would be thinking that I am not good enough to be Jean's new wife and Kateri's step-mother. But then I realized he was speaking to me.

"*Kwe, Kwe.*" Hello, my daughter. And with that, I was welcomed into Jean's Mohawk family.

The chattering began then, with names exchanged as I was introduced to Kateri's grandmother and to her cousin and his wife, who held a small baby in her arms. This sleeping cubicle was to be ours, Kateri told me; the three of us would share it, as was the custom of Mohawk families.

Then I noticed a man, one who was not *indien*, who was standing away from everyone, his arms folded across his chest, a wide smile on his face. Someone taken in war and adopted into the family? I wondered.

"Madame," said the man. "I am no prisoner, but live here willingly, helping Père Raffeix and acting as his interpreter." Bowing, he added that he was Charles Boquet, and that he was contracted to the Jesuits. He and Jean must hunt tomorrow if the cooking pots in this longhouse were to be filled to the satisfaction of the women.

They did, and how we feasted. Even Père Raffeix joined us.

Le 16 décembre 1667

Yet another bitterly cold day. The longhouse is nothing like our home in Montréal, but it is warm enough. Still, I am glad that I wear two *chemises*, two pairs of stockings, skirts — two of everything.

The work — I am husking corn — gives me time to think about how we are living here. One of the *cabanes* is the chapel and the residence of Père Raffeix, Charles Boquet and some of the *indiens* converts. The other houses two families of *habitants* from Montréal. They are very crowded there, I must say. In the large longhouses are a mixture of Oneida and Mohawk people, also converts. But in the small longhouse, our longhouse, only Jean, Kateri and I have been baptized. All of Kateri's family follow the old ways, and in fact seem suspicious of some of the things that Père Raffeix tries to tell them. Jean says that it is a wise thing to make such an important decision as baptism carefully. Perhaps.

I can again hear the singing coming from Père Raffeix's house. We have been told that they are practising for Midnight Mass. I do not recognize the hymn, though.

Le 18 décembre 1667

Kateri's cousin is called Sonhatsi. His wife is Atiron. Their baby, who has no name yet, and whom we simply call Owira, or Baby, has a bad cough. It is at its worst at night, and the smokiness of the longhouse does not help at all. I will make the baby a poultice of wild onions to help soothe her.

Tard

The wind has risen horribly until now it is shrieking around the longhouse, drowning out Owira's coughing. I am reminded of the terrible storm through which we sailed here to New France.

No. I will not write of such things.

Le 19 décembre 1667

The storm continues. No one ventures outside the palisade for fear of becoming lost in the heavy, blowing snow. I am now also coughing and so is Kateri.

Le 21 décembre 1667

This morning it was necessary for Jean and the other men to tunnel through the snowdrift that had blocked one of the openings that serves as the long-house's two doors. When the air blew in, the cold made me shiver, but it also made me realize how strongly this longhouse smells of smoke.

We are to depart the mission in the morning if the storm has ended. I will miss Kateri's family, but look forward to the smells of my own kitchen.

Dear Jean. Sensing this, he cut and brought in fresh spruce boughs for the sleeping platforms. How wonderful they smell!

Tard la nuit

Poor Owira. In the night she began to suffer from a high fever and now is having difficulty breathing. I will keep my fears for her to myself.

Plus tard

Jean and Kateri — I can hide nothing from them, since they see it all on my face. Jean has sent Charles with a message to Tante Barbe. He will go as quickly as he can through the storm.

We will remain here at the mission.

Le 23 décembre 1667

Père Raffeix came and prayed over the baby, which Owira's parents permitted, but when he whispered to Jean of baptism, my husband shook his head, saying that now was not the time to speak of such things. I said nothing, but if the baby should die . . . Jean spoke briefly of a sweat lodge, but the storm makes that impossible.

I have tried to think of what else may be done. There is something I once saw Tante Barbe do when a little boy was ill and could not breathe, and so I have set water to boiling and found a clean blanket to drape over the baby and her

Plus tard

Tante Barbe is here! She has been pulled the entire way on a *traîne* by Charles and the Cavalier de la Salle, who came along for the adventure! At first I did not recognize her, she was so covered in snow! We wept when she pulled me into her arms. She was certain that my health as well as dear Kateri's must be in danger, in spite of Charles's assurances.

"I was wrong," she said in relief, dabbing at her eyes with the corner of her apron. "You two suffer only from colds. But this poor child!" And in a flash she was kneeling next to the baby. Then she hugged me again, saying that I was a clever girl to remember what must be done. She had packets of herbs with her and so she put hyssop and lavender into the boiling water. With Jean's and Sonhatsi's help the steaming kettle was placed in front of Owira's mother, who had the baby in her arms. The blanket was draped over them both so that the soothing steam would loosen the baby's breathing.

Ákhsot nodded and observed that our idea was a good one, that the cloth tent would act as a sweat lodge. There was no more to do but pray, and so I told my beads, closing my eyes so that I would not be distracted, but a sound caused me to open them. It was Ákhsot, who was also praying. Later Kateri explained that her grandmother had been praying to The Master of Life, which is how they refer to *le bon Dieu*. Prayer and the good medicines of Tante Barbe — surely mercy will be shown to this little one.

Le 24 décembre 1667

What a gift. The baby's coughing and breathing have eased. And yet a second gift. Not only will Tante Barbe be here with us this Christmas, so shall Ourson! Charles was only waiting until the crisis had passed before he brought Ourson in from Père Raffeix's *cabane,* where he had been given shelter from the storm.

"There was no question of bringing the cats, and so those two have remained at the inn with Seraphim," huffed Tante Barbe. "He spoils rather than disciplines the wicked creatures! Minette and Sottise have twice taken the shepherds from my *crèche* . . . and the angels — they no longer resemble angels!"

I had to hide my smiles, but could not help wondering that surely there might have been cats and even a dog in the stable on this night so long ago.

Plus tard

The longhouse sleeps around us. Only Jean is awake, watching as I write.

The mass tonight was lovely. Not even the fierce wind could drown out the sounds of the choir. The sweetest song they sang? One in the Huron language, a hymn called "*Iesous Ahatonhia,* Jesus Is Born." They say it was written by Père Jean de Brébeuf, a Jesuit missionary who was killed almost twenty years ago, during a war fought between the Iroquois and the Huron.

What a blessing is this peace among all of us.

Le 25 décembre 1667

Joyeux Noël!

We had a Christmas feast of stew, corn soup and savory *tourtières* that Tante Barbe had brought secretly from home and kept wrapped and hidden until now. La Salle and Charles spent hours talking about the cavalier's plans to explore the west. Jean listened with great interest, but it did not alarm me. He has no wish to live the life of an adventurer, he once said. Life at home is adventure enough.

We will exchange small gifts on New Year's Day, as is the custom, once we are back in Montréal. And yet I have been given a gift here today by Kateri's grandmother, for it is she who has given me a Mohawk name! Ionattokha'. She says I am to be known this way when among them. Its meaning made me blush when Jean explained.

"Well, She Is Wise," he teased me, "the storm has passed, the baby is healing and my family talks of returning to their own village. Are you ready to face the journey home?"

Oui! I answered him. I do not feel particularly wise, but perhaps in time I may come to live up to my name. Until then, I am wise enough to know that the life we have together is a wonderful gift.

Isobel Scott

Footsteps in the Snow
The Red River Diary of Isobel Scott
Rupert's Land
July 1815 – July 1817

By Carol Matas

*Along with other Selkirk settlers who
struggled to reach the Red River Settlement after their
long voyage from Scotland, Isobel Scott and her family
must again leave The Forks to winter elsewhere —
this time, as once before, at Fort Daer.*

Shelter from the Cold

December 1, 1817

I am fed up! Yes, diary, I dare to write these words here, although as you can well imagine, I dare not utter them aloud. I am fed up and more! Everyone is at everyone else's throat. Fighting, bickering, sniping, short tempers, furrowed eyebrows, glowering looks — that is the state of our household. Only Father rises above it; indeed he barely notices, which is one of the problems. White Loon is in her early months with child and she is lethargic and can keep no food down at all. Father is worried about her and their child, and constantly fusses over her when he is home. Otherwise he is out hunting with White Loon's father every day. James too is out hunting and returns home tired and grumpy.

This is the third year that we have been forced to leave The Forks and winter elsewhere. Once again we are at Ft. Daer, living in small huts, and there is little in the way of comfort or food. To top it off, we seem to have acquired a ghost! There are strange noises at night, food is disappearing, and Kate swears we are being visited by a poltergeist. Robbie has stopped sleeping, he is so frightened, and somehow I am supposed to keep everyone happy, healthy, eating well, sleeping well and getting along well. It's hopeless!

Mother was always so good at keeping the peace, whereas I seem to only add to the troubles. It is at times like these I feel her loss acutely.

December 3

This morning began with shrieks of terror from Kate. As we were taking off our nightclothes, small white lights shot out from the clothes, illuminating the darkness around us. I remember the same thing happening last winter, although we never discovered the reason. I must admit it was a bit frightening. She began to wail that it was her poor father, murdered last year near Seven Oaks, come back to haunt her. She shed no tears but screamed in such an eerie way that even I had goosebumps.

As for Robbie, he threw on his clothes and sprinted from the hut without any breakfast. Still, he shan't go hungry. His friends will be sure he eats — that's all the young lads do, it seems, eat. And us with so little food! But somehow whatever is to be had they find a way to get into their stomachs. I had to make a calming tea for Kate and another one for White Loon to help her stomach, make a fire — my nostrils closing in on themselves all the while, it is so cold — and get the porridge on for Father and James. By the time that was done I had to sweep out the hut, shake out the blankets, beat the pillows, scrub the pots and start dinner.

Finally White Loon made me take a rest. I went outside to a white landscape, a blue sky, and a cold so fierce it made me cough every time I took a breath. Still I was glad for a small respite from housework. Kate and I walked around the huts, meeting others of our age, including Alice, who merely glanced at Kate and then pretended she did not exist. Kate could not resist tormenting her, knowing full well that Alice is mad for James and means to marry him.

"Oh, it is such a delight to be living with your family," Kate said to me. "Especially under the *same* roof as James. To watch him work at night on his necklaces and bracelets is nothing short of inspiring."

Alice appeared ready to explode. Her face turned bright red like an over-filled skin. Can she not see how Kate is baiting her? She put her arm through mine and walked ahead of Kate, leaving her to trail behind. At that point we encountered Robbie and

Peter and a group of four other boys. They had just finished piling snow up against the door of a hut so whoever was inside would be unable to get out. I put my hand on my hips and glared at them. They meekly undid their mischief. I realize that I must start to take better care of Robbie. I had been schooling him over the summer, but since we've been here have been far too busy. And I supposed there was no time like the present, so without pause I said, "You lads follow me, now."

We returned to our small hut and I settled everyone on the floor. The other girls sat near me and we took turns reading to the boys. Father had managed to obtain a copy of *The Swiss Family Robinson* from The Hudson's Bay Company store. I know it is not the Bible, but it is written by a pastor, and it teaches wonderful values, telling a story of a family who must rely on each other and be resourceful to survive. How similar to our plight! I must say that the children were fascinated, as were the older girls, and we had a lovely hour together. But then, back to work for everyone.

December 4

I begin to fear that there is a thief amongst us! Food is definitely disappearing. And sometimes the door is found open, allowing the most frightful drafts into the hut. Father says it needs fixing as it isn't closing properly. Or could we really have a ghost?

December 5

When I sleep I hear whimpering and crying. But when I get up and move, it stops. Kate really believes it is her dead Father. She couldn't eat a bite of food today and paced up and down outdoors all day, despite the bitter cold. I fear her sanity could be giving way. I have mentioned it to White Loon, who thinks perhaps it is a restless spirit.

Father says we are imagining things — he can hear nothing.

Robbie was kept busy all of today helping out at the Cree encampment. White Loon's brothers needed the younger boys' help tending the dogs.

December 8

It is a *dog!* I caught it this morning. I heard the sounds, crept out ever so quietly and there it was! It has a broken leg, I believe, and has somehow been living off scraps it has found when we were out or sleeping. Actually it is a she. And she has the sweetest eyes you could ever imagine. She looked up at me in the most trusting manner and with a mute plea for help.

But if she is so trusting, why not present herself in the open? It is a mystery. I need to find out more before I act, so I will ask White Loon about the tribe's dogs. I know very little about them except that some are noble and beautiful, some quite terrifying. But they are all hard workers. Will the dog, injured as she is, be put to death if I expose her?

December 9

I have named her Cocoa. She is a mixed colour of dark brown and light brown. Her muzzle is a light, almost reddish brown, her eyes the colour of tree bark.

I have made her a bed scooped out of the snow at the back of the hut in a hollow where it is unlikely anyone will notice her. How she remained so invisible to everyone I have no idea.

I asked White Loon about the dogs in the camp. Most are working dogs, trained to pull sleds. Some are trained to watch the children. Some are also pets. I asked her what would happen to a sick animal. White Loon said that it depended on its owner. She was feeling particularly unwell, so I couldn't press her further. In fact I needed to make her some tea and force her to stop cooking and cleaning. She had decided that sitting about was not the Indian way and revolted against Father's demands for her to rest. But her illness got the better of her and she was forced to sit down and confine herself to mending our moccasins for the even colder weather ahead.

I need to find out where this dog belongs without giving too much away. After all, if the dog — Cocoa — if Cocoa loved her owner, wouldn't she have stayed with him? I fear that she has run away for a reason.

I need to fix her leg but am unsure how.

December 11

I have managed to set Cocoa's leg, with help from Mother's trusty little book on medicinal remedies. It's not exactly like a human leg but I think I have managed, using some old woolen strips and sewing it all tightly on the leg. She allowed me to do it with barely a cry. Honestly, she must be the bravest dog in the whole world. She waits patiently for me in the morning and no longer raids our kitchen, knowing that I will provide for her.

It hasn't been easy keeping her a secret from Robbie in particular, but I fear that if he discovers her it will be all over the camp in two shakes and then her owner might demand her return. There is a little voice inside me that worries — what if her owner is devoted to her and is missing her and I am keeping them apart?

December 12

It is getting too cold to leave her outside. I am going to have to bring her in. This morning she was almost frozen.

Later

I brought Cocoa into the house and it caused such an uproar I cannot even begin to describe it in these pages, but I will try! First of all Robbie: he danced about her as if she were a unicorn. I have never seen such a fuss in my life, but it was very sweet. He cuddled her and petted her and spoke to her as if she understood every word he said — including gentle scolding for scaring him and making him think we had a ghost in the house.

James seemed to not care one way or another. He has become so busy with hunting every day, and game is so scarce because of the cold, that he is too tired to care about anything.

Kate was unimpressed to say the least. "Surely, we aren't going to try to stretch our food to include *this* beast?" she demanded.

I glared at her, ready to kill her right there on the spot, but the damage was done and Father agreed with her!

"She has a point," he said. "We barely have enough for us all."

But it was White Loon's reaction that worried me the most. "Isobel," she said, "that is a beautiful animal. It must belong to someone. Shouldn't you find out who?"

That is what I feared most about bringing her in, but had I left her outdoors she certainly would have frozen to death. "What if her owner wants to kill her?" I said. "She isn't of any use anymore."

White Loon thought for a moment, then said it wasn't up to me, and that I must do the right thing and return her to her rightful owner.

I turned to Father. "But her owner might kill her!"

Father paused for a moment and then said that he would think it over. It was definitely a problem that needed some thought.

At least she is cuddled up beside me now and snoring happily.

December 15

It is becoming almost impossible to keep Cocoa a secret. Robbie's friends were in the shack today for another reading and some more schooling. We hid Cocoa in her spot behind the shed but she wasn't happy and whined to come in. We had to pretend we didn't hear anything when the children asked what the noise was, and then Robbie declared that we had a ghost!

Well, the children became nervous and frightened and could barely sit still for their lessons. I stared daggers at Robbie, but he was having such a wonderful time playing this joke on his friends that he ignored me completely and played it up even more. One of the boys was reduced to tears and I had to stop the class and allow the boys out to play. I think Robbie has just discovered another way to avoid study!

December 16

A disaster! James took me aside after the meal tonight to talk to me. He thinks he knows whom the dog belongs to — one of the fiercest hunters in the tribe. James heard him complain the other day that his favourite hunting dog had been injured and then gone missing before he could deal with her. I asked what he meant by "deal with her," but James said that was all Red Fox had said. I asked if he couldn't find out more, but he pointed out that if he did that, he would also have to tell Red Fox where his dog was, or lose honour. In fact, he said that if White Loon found out that we know who the owner is, she would be sure to make me return Cocoa.

December 17

Kate is blackmailing me! She told me that she is going to find out who the owner is and give the dog back. She said that Cocoa eats too much and that James — yes, James — is not getting enough food. She is worried about him. He is looking pale and drawn and somehow she blames the dog! She says that I either find a way to get more food into the house or she will give up the dog. How can I find us more food?

December 18

I have gone to the Hudson's Bay store and offered my extra pair of moccasins for some porridge and flour. We were definitely low on both and everyone was making do with half portions over the last week. If Father finds out he will be so angry I dread to think. He'll feel I've brought disgrace on the family. And I certainly hope White Loon doesn't discover this, since she made me an extra pair only after I pleaded with her, telling her I needed them because my old ones were getting too small. I know only too well that these were to go to Kate, who will grow into them all too soon. How am I to explain this extra food? It seems that I am going from one trouble to another.

December 19

Kate was very happy with the extra rations this morning and looked at James with a small smile as he wolfed down every spoonful. I kept up a desperate chatter with Father and White Loon so they wouldn't notice that everyone's bowls were much fuller than normal. I must admit that I put just a little less in theirs so they would not notice. (That was easy with White Loon, as she can barely hold down any food and asks me to give her only a little.)

December 20

Another near miss, Dear Diary, and this one very scary! Red Fox went through our camp today looking for Cocoa. I could hear someone calling outside so I peeked out the door and there he was walking about and calling as loud as could be. And here is the amazing part. She cowered under the table and shook! Yes, it's true! She obviously understood quite well that he was looking for her and she refused to go to him. That tells me that he must have been cruel to her and it also explains why she ran away. I cannot give her back! But now that he is searching for her, how much longer can she stay? She hobbles around now quite nicely, by the way, and has become extremely fond of everyone in the house — even Kate, much to Kate's chagrin. When anyone walks in she licks them all over. She plays ball with Robbie out back and can hobble after it at quite a pace, bringing it faithfully back to him. But the sweetest thing is that she seems to know that White Loon is with child, because at night when White Loon sits on a fur rug near the fire, Cocoa lies beside her with her head on White Loon's stomach! It is almost as if she is protecting the child already. And although Cocoa is a hunter, White Loon tells me that when the men were out hunting and the women would also need to leave the camp to gather berries and such, some dogs would take care of the children.

December 21

Kate is going to betray me! She announced at dinner that it is wrong for us to be harbouring this animal and that we must return it. Robbie almost hit her, he was so angry! James looked at her in a puzzled way, unable to fathom why she should feel so strongly. He has no idea that she has decided that Cocoa is stealing the very food from his mouth.

(And me in shock having no idea that she felt like this about him, no idea at all! If Alice, who set her sights on James from the first moment she noticed him, finds out, there really will be trouble!) Father reluctantly agreed with Kate. He said that we must make an effort to discover the owner. James looked at me sideways, but gave nothing away. I am convinced that Cocoa will be killed if we return her, as she will never again be fast enough to be a good hunter. Had she been a pet it might be different. On the other hand, to be fair, how can I know this for certain? Perhaps Red Fox has a family and they are attached to Cocoa — as attached as I am. Then again, if that is true, why did Cocoa cower like that when she heard Red Fox calling her name?

I need to find out. I must make a foray into the camp.

December 22

I convinced White Loon that it has been too long since she has visited with her mother and that we should go to their camp. We set off after breakfast. The day was clear and cold. We left Cocoa inside, and Kate was also left to do chores that White Loon set her. It was quite a walk to the camp. White Loon told me that soon the camp would be moving as it did last year, to follow the buffalo, and we would probably move with them again too. Frankly, I look forward to it. Living in tents is no colder than the huts, and far less work. And I loved the games we played and the respite from the daily chores. The work when the buffalo were killed was fierce, but the play made up for it all.

We were received warmly by Leaf Bud and we sat with her in her tent, trading stories and news. My Cree is very good now and I can understand most things, although I cannot express myself that well.

White Loon brought up the dog very casually, mentioning that she had seen a dog in our camp that seemed to belong to no one. Leaf Bud immediately exclaimed that it must be Red Fox's dog — it had hurt itself while hunting and slunk away. I asked if Red Fox had a family that would miss the dog. She laughed and answered no, that Red Fox only cared because he spent many hours training this dog and wanted it back so he did not have to work so hard again.

Inside, I sighed with relief. But I should not have. White Loon said that anyone finding the dog would be bound by honour to return it and her mother agreed. What was I to do?

We were in for quite a shock when we returned home. Kate was weeping when we walked into the hut. Now, dear Diary, you know very well that Kate *never* weeps! I was so taken aback that at first I didn't know how to react. White Loon rushed over to her and took her hand. "What has happened?" she asked.

"I was attacked by a coyote when I went to get water," Kate replied, showing bite marks on one arm and deep scratches on both. White Loon tried to hide her concern but we all know that a bite from an animal can fester and kill. On the other hand, Kate could have been killed outright. I was about to ask her how she survived when she said, "Cocoa saved me."

I whirled around to look for Cocoa, my heart in my throat. Was she dead? Had she sacrificed herself for Kate?

"Where is she?" I asked.

"Out back, guarding the hut," Kate answered. "I was worried about Robbie and his friends being attacked when they came home, so I left her outside."

White Loon gave me no time to check on Cocoa. We had to treat Kate's wound right away. I gathered the herbs from the small larder we had organized and we pummelled them together and made a poultice to put on the open wounds. Then White Loon made a tea from birchbark and made sure Kate drank it all down. She washed Kate's arms with snow and made sure that they were as clean as possible before we applied the poultice. Kate's face was white as the snow, as she realized the danger she was in. When all was done I hurried to the back and found Cocoa, who was sitting up, alert and watchful. I gave her a big hug and told her to stay and watch out for Robbie.

That night when James and Father had returned from the hunt with three rabbits and I had cleaned and cooked them and we had all eaten until full, we discussed Cocoa and Kate's close call. Father declared that we had a true dilemma. We were honour bound to return the dog, and yet we had found a true friend in Cocoa and no one, now not even Kate, wanted to give her up.

Then I had an idea. Handsel Monday was only two weeks away. I made a suggestion. "I would happily give up any present you were going to give me," I said. "You could instead give it to Red Fox. My present would be keeping Cocoa."

In no time Robbie, James — and yes, even Kate — had chimed in and made the same offer.

"I have little enough money to spend, but I could pool what I have and buy a small knife at the store," Father said. "Are you all certain this is what you want?"

We all were.

Now we only need to wait and see if Red Fox will agree.

January 5, 1818

Cocoa is ours! I am sorry I have not written, but we have been so busy. Kate developed a fever and was very sick. I have been nursing her constantly until last night, when suddenly her eyes cleared and her fever broke and she announced that she was starving. Father needed time to make a deal with the manager at the store, but finally yesterday he travelled to the Indian camp and offered Red Fox the knife in exchange for his dog. Red Fox was a little suspicious about how long we had had the dog, but Father managed to convince him that at first we did not know who the owner was. Red Fox did accept in the end, and today was the most wonderful beginning of the New Year. Cocoa is officially my dog now! But everyone in the family loves her and I have no doubt she will continue to protect us and take care of us. And here is a strange thing — the bickering and misery we were all prone to only weeks ago has now been replaced by games with Cocoa of an evening, or a scramble to see who will cuddle up with her for the night. A good start to the New Year indeed.

Marianna Wilson

Orphan at My Door
The Home Child Diary of Victoria Cope
Guelph, Ontario
May 1897 – September 1897

By Jean Little

Marianna Wilson, one of thousands of Home Children sent from British orphanages to Canada by philanthropist Dr. Thomas Barnardo, lives with the Cope family in Ontario. Marianna now has a diary of her own, courtesy of her friend Victoria.

A Home Girl's Christmas

Friday evening, December 2, 1898

Victoria Cope gave me this notebook to use as a diary when I told her she had inspired me to keep one. She let me read hers first. It was a little strange to read all about Jasper and me coming here a year and a half ago and everything that happened to us after we arrived from Dr. Barnardo's Homes in England. She said I should wait until New Year's Day to begin but I am not going to. I can't wait that long to blow off steam about Sadie Harris. The things she has said to me are troubling my mind. I cannot discuss her with Victoria because poor Sadie needs people to be nice to her and, if Vic knew what S. thinks, she might hold it against her.

The weeks leading up to Christmas could be sad ones as I think of my own mother and my little lost sister. When Jasper and our baby sister (the first Emily Rose) and I were sent to Canada we didn't know what to expect. But Dr. and Mrs. Cope are kind to me. (Not like David, their oldest son.) Tom and Vic treat me like one of the family. And of course there is baby Rosie, named after my real sister, Emily Rose.

I wonder where my own Emily Rose is now. We never even met the couple who adopted her, and we were given no chance to tell them anything about our family. Mam would not have wanted her to be taken away from us, but there was nothing I could do to stop them. The Barnardo people just kept saying our mother had died and they were thinking what was best for our baby. Nobody gave me a chance to say what I thought until she was gone. I could not think it out either. But I believe our baby should know about Mam and her family in England and also be able to find Jasper and me if she needs us. What the young think doesn't count, though. I am old enough to work as hard as any grown woman, but that doesn't count either. It is bitter to be a child at such a time.

I hope Victoria does not ask to read this diary. She has too soft a heart to be faced with the hardships we have been through.

Yet all this is not what I want to write about. I want to put down what Sadie Harris said to me at school and how it stung. I'll have to do it tomorrow, though. I am too tired to write it all down tonight. Barnardo girls, or Home Girls as some call us, get up early to light the stove and get the breakfast started. I can think while I'm putting the porridge on and fetching in kindling, but I cannot write.

Saturday, December 3

Sadie is a Home Girl too, a skinny little thing with a pinched, pale face. Her skin is the colour of a raw potato. Her cheeks don't ever grow pink and her lips are thin and look almost bloodless. Molly, the other Home Girl in our class, heard that Sadie came from the poorhouse, and I can tell anyone who asks that children in the poorhouse get no good food. I know how awful it is — thin gruel, dry bread, cabbage cooked until it is limp and no longer green. "This thing has forgotten it was ever a cabbage," Mam said the day before she took us away and put us in Dr. Barnardo's orphans' home. It was only supposed to be until she could earn enough money to take us back.

You would think all this would make me and Sadie Harris friends, but it does not. Feeling pity for someone does not make you *like* the person.

It even makes you angry at her because it is such a rasping sort of feeling, rubbing your heart raw. I do not want to lose my memories of those terrible days, but I wish the pain would go out of them the way an old scar stops hurting even though you can still rub it and picture the wound. If the pain went away entirely, though, perhaps I would not be able to call up Mam's face and the way her fingers felt when she took hold of the back of my neck and gave it a gentle shake. "Enough of that, girl," she would say.

When I look at Sadie, I feel as though I have swallowed a file and it is stuck inside me, rubbing up and down. Sadie's nose is sharp and her eyes are a washed-out blue. Her hair is light brown like brown sugar. It is always dragged back into a knot which makes her look like a little old woman instead of a child. She works for a bedridden woman who orders Sadie around from her couch. The law says she has to send Sadie to school, but she only lets her come when she has done all her morning chores. Sadie usually arrives around ten or even eleven and has to be back at the woman's house by three. The teacher should tell the woman that Sadie needs more time in school, but that does not happen when the person is a Home Child.

I have never seen S. smile. The other day, I began talking to her about our lives before we came here and she pulled me away into a corner of the schoolyard where nobody could overhear. Then she told me that I am not to say she was ever at Barnardo's. She is telling people she is an orphan whose parents died in a fire. She has a whole story made up about how her father owned his own shop in Bath but it burned down and she was left an orphan. As soon as she is old enough to escape and has saved up some money, she plans to run off and make a fresh start, and she is not going to tell anyone she was ever at Barnardo's. She says she won't tell her husband, when she gets one, or her children. I asked her why and she just looked at me in her cold scornful way and said she is ashamed of being a Home Girl.

I can tell she really lived down by the docks in London and she spoke Cockney just like most of us. But she is studying how to speak proper. I told her I saw nothing to be ashamed of and neither does Molly, who came from Barnardo's too, or Jasper.

She sniffed and asked if I had been treated like a member of the family or like a slavey. I started to say just like a member of the family and then I remembered David calling us "scum" at first. He is still pretty cool sometimes.

"I knew it," Sadie said with a cat's pounce. "So you keep away from me, Mary Anna Wilson. I am going to better myself, and being friends with you won't do me any good."

She knows my name is Marianna, like the girl in Tennyson's poem, but she always says Mary and then Anna. I know she thinks it is a common name.

Then she rapped out a vulgar question that showed how common she is herself. "Who is the richest girl in here?"

"Prue," I told her and walked away.

Prue Bellingham won't have anything to do with Sadie even if Sadie never drops another *h*. Prue's mother never lets her mix with lesser folk. I feel as sorry for Prue as I do for Sadie. Her mother's as stiff as Dr. Cope's shirts were when Victoria put in double the amount of starch. Unbending. Prue never dares sit on the grass for fear of staining her skirt and she always has two clean handkerchiefs in her pocket.

And I am ashamed that I dislike both her and Sadie, the poor things, but I do. Toplofty, uppity, nose-in-the-air prigs.

That is enough about Sadie. I just had to get down how she made me feel before it exploded like the bottle of ginger beer Jasper hid in the cellar and forgot.

Sunday afternoon, December 4

I have had my diary for three days now, but it was talking to Sadie that made me need to begin writing in it. The thing that makes it so strange is that I am not ashamed of who I am or where I come from, and yet deep inside, I understand Sadie's struggle. You feel you are in a race with a lot of other girls, but you have a sharp, heavy stone in your shoe and you cannot get it out and you begin to fall behind. I know I have fallen behind where I might be if I were really Victoria's flesh-and-blood sister. The Copes are wonderfully kind to us, except for David sometimes, but nobody *needs* to be kind to Victoria. My mam would say she was born with a silver spoon in her mouth.

Right now, Vic is so busy practising her piece for the Christmas concert that she doesn't notice I have started writing in my notebook. This year she is not only in a tableau but she is playing the piano. She loves being in the tableau but she hates the piano. She even calls her piano teacher Miss Hopeless instead of her proper name, Miss Hope. (And she calls the piece she's practising "Humersquee." It is really called "Humoresque," I think.) How I envy her those wonderful piano lessons she so abominates!

Once in a while, when the family are all out, I press down the keys ever so gently and pick out bits of tunes. Even when I have to stop, I hear the notes playing on inside my heart. Sometimes I pretend I am playing scales, as Victoria does, but I do it on the edge of the table or on my quilt in bed. I wish I could have lessons. My father used to play the concertina long ago and he let me press the keys sometimes. I used to sing too. Mam said I was "full of music," but that was in a lost time. I am so seldom alone now. And there is always housework I should be doing. After all, nice as they are to me, I am still their Home Girl. I am never reminded of it outright, but they do not look at me as another Victoria. Aunt Lily counts on me, though, in a way she never counts on Vic. When something goes wrong, I am the one she calls to help her.

Monday, December 5

Victoria's being so busy has even little Rosie feeling neglected, and every time any one of us sits down, Victoria's pug dog Snortle is up on our laps with a leap. Usually Victoria's lap is ready and waiting, but not just now.

Something exciting did happen today. Emily Rose Cope said my name. Well, she meant it to be my name. "Mawina" was what she actually said. She calls Victoria "Bicky" as though she is a gingersnap. Mawina and Bicky don't mind. Rosie has no word for David yet, even though he is sweet as pie to her. I should not be pleased about this, but he was so nasty to me and Jasper when we first arrived that I cannot help gloating. He is decent to us now, but I doubt he has ever said good morning to any of the other Barnardo children who have been settled in Guelph. Tom has always been friendly. It is strange how different two brothers can be.

Snortle attacked the neighbour's Pekingese. He came off the winner but that little dog stuck up for herself. They did look so funny with their little black faces glaring. Until I came here, I never knew a pug dog and I think I looked down my nose at the idea of such pets, but Victoria's Snortle persuaded me that pugs are the best canines going.

Time to peel the potatoes for dinner. Victoria is a poor potato peeler. She digs out half the potato along with the eye. I have wondered, now and then, if she does this on purpose so the job will be passed on to me, Marianna Wilson, champion potato peeler. But I do not really believe she is quite that much of a schemer. Her conscience would not allow her to keep it up even if she has done it now and then. I am proud of my potato peelings. You can practically see through them. And Aunt Lily taught me to peel one long apple peeling and let it tell my fortune. It is supposed to tell you the initial of the man you will marry some-day. But if the apples know something, I'm going to marry a crowd.

Uncle Alastair is planning something nasty and I do not like the sound of it. I was not supposed to hear. He told Aunt Lily that something came today and he will do Rosie and me and Jasper tomorrow. She asked if we'd be better by Christmas and he said, "Of course!" What on earth can he be talking about? I cannot think of any one thing that you would give a girl of fourteen, a boy of nine and a baby of one and a half. It does not sound pleasant. I asked Victoria and she thought it was some sort of special treat and began by being jealous. Then she said she would try to find out.

Later the same night

Uncle A. is going to vaccinate us against the smallpox! I don't want to have it done but I don't want to get the smallpox either. The vaccine gives you a disease. Cowpox, my mam said once. She thought it was dangerous. "No child of mine is being given a dangerous illness on purpose," she told the matron.

But I know right now that Uncle A. won't listen to what she said. I am afraid.

Victoria showed me her vaccination scar. It looks like a white circle, a bit bumpy, and ugly, but it is hidden under her sleeve most of the time.

Nessie Smye had the smallpox and her face was so pockmarked that people looked away when she passed. I don't want that. I have also known children to die of smallpox. And adults too. In the poorhouse, seven of the inmates died shortly before we left and Mam heard the matron say, "Good riddance." (The whole saying is "Good riddance to bad rubbish," but even Matron did not go that far in speaking of human beings.)

I snuggled Rosie especially close tonight when I put her to bed. She has not one scar on her beautiful little body. And she is such a cheerful baby. Hardly ever ailing. I wonder how her father can bear to hurt her. No wonder women don't become doctors. Some actually want to. I have decided I might be a nurse, though. Dr. Graham told me I would make a good one when I helped care for Victoria's Great-Aunt Lib before she died, and also when I helped out at Rosie's birth.

Wednesday afternoon, December 7

He did it. I planned to tell him what Mam said, but he did not let me finish. He told me he knew my mother would want me to have it done. He started with me so Jasper could see what would happen. Uncle A. scratched my arm with something sharp. I didn't look until he finished that bit. Then he swabbed the scratch with this vaccine. Then I had to wait, holding out my arm, until the stuff dried. I wanted to ask if he had given me cowpox, but Jasper's eyes were enormous and he had gone white as butter-milk, so I decided to hold my whisht and be utterly brave.

Jasper was brave but he did come close to swooning.

"Buck up," I told him. "Think of the Spartans." He likes that boy who let a fox eat his "vitals" without complaining. I can't imagine anyone really could do this. But it helped Jasper. He looked daggers at me and bit his lip hard and held his arm out steady as a rock.

Then Aunt Lily fetched Emily Rose Cope. She was laughing and so sweet. I saw, all at once, that Aunt Lily was about to faint, so I reached out and took the baby and held her all through the procedure. Aunt Lily ran out of the room. She must have been ashamed of herself, I think, because as soon as Rosie began howling, she came running back. How that poor baby did howl!

Uncle A. looked at me and said, so seriously, "Marianna, I've thought before that you would make a fine nurse, and this convinces me. You think it over."

So I am thinking. I know that you have to go and live in a nurses' residence next to the hospital and you work for your board and room while you study. But I am used to that sort of work, washing floors and dumping chamber pots and cleaning up messes and carrying trays. I have done that sort of work ever since I was a little thing and, after Jasper was born and our mother was so sick, I did nearly everything even though I was still only six years old. Then, when our sister Emily Rose was born and we went into the poorhouse, I never had five minutes free.

Sadie may think her life here in Canada is hard, but I know it is better than the one she had in the poor-house.

Thursday, December 8

My arm is all hot and swollen and it throbs. They say "it took" when it gets like mine. A big scab has formed over the place where I was vaccinated and I cannot sleep. I tiptoed down the hall to the boys' room to check on Jasper, but he is sleeping like a baby. His arm was on top of the covers, and although it is a bit warmer than usual, it is not like mine. Maybe it didn't "take." If it is to guard you against the smallpox, you have to have a reaction showing you really got a dose of cowpox. I got one for sure. I must go back to bed, I suppose, but I don't know how I can bear this through all the hours until morning.

I was back in my room when I heard Rosie begin to cry. She is so sick. I went creeping down to her crib and I found Aunt Lily trying to soothe her. But you just have to look at her baby cheeks, so flushed and burning to touch. Her eyes are wide and she did not know me. Aunt Lily looked sick herself. I went and brewed up some camomile tea for the two of us and when I brought it, I made Aunt Lily hand her over.

"I can't sleep either," I said and I showed her my arm.

She actually began to cry over us. She is so tired. I wonder if she is in the family way again. I hope not. Rosie's birth was hard on her and she has four children now plus that baby who died long ago.

Anyway, I walked up and down and sang to Rosie until she slept, but her rest is fretful and she needs watching. My mother used to sing to us a song called "All through the night," which talked about "I, my loving vigil keeping." Aunt Lily woke Uncle Alastair and he gave me some laudanum and sent me to bed. But I am writing in here because I still can't sleep. He looked at my arm and seemed to think it was fine! I can feel my heart thumping away, but maybe the laudanum is beginning to work because everything is growing a bit fuzzy.

Wednesday, December 14

We have all recovered, even Rosie. Jasper's vaccination did not bother him nearly as much as ours, but Uncle Alastair thinks it was enough to protect him if we have an outbreak of smallpox. I hope he is right. Jasper has freckles. He does not need to add pockmarks to his spotty little face.

Now that Dr. Cope thinks I can train as a nurse someday, he takes time to explain medical things to me. It is nice to be treated respectfully, as though I am another adult.

Monday, December 19

I have not had time to write in here because we are so busy doing Christmas baking. We made the puddings today. Such a performance! When night comes, I fall onto my bed and sleep instantly.

Friday, December 23

Last night, we all went to the school and saw the tableaux. Victoria was Florence Nightingale and Molly was Laura Secord. I thought there should be a live cow for Molly to lead through the enemy lines, but I knew better than to say so. Victoria looked clean and neat and spiritual even though she let her lamp wobble a couple of times. The audience gasped. But she grinned and steadied it again. But I'll bet Miss Nightingale, when she nursed soldiers during the Crimean War, was not so spick and span. Those hospitals were terrible places!

Sadie was going on and on about Florence Nightingale being English like us. I'm proud of our British heroine too. Yet I believe I am starting to feel more Canadian. Sadie makes me squirm with her boasting about the "Motherland." It was not so wonderfully mothering to me and Jasper.

Sadie is going to be leaving right at New Year's. She

told us after the concert. She looked paler than pastry dough and she actually had tears in her eyes. The old woman she was helping to care for died and the family do not need her any longer. I hoped she would go somewhere genteel, but she has been told she is being packed off to a farm north of Arthur.

I do wish her luck. Maybe she will discover she loves the country, but most Home Children do not. They have to work so hard and nobody understands what a shock a farm is when you have spent all your life in London. It is dirty enough in the slums, but it is not at all like farm dirt. It smells human. Before coming out here, most Home Children have never seen a cow, let alone milked one, or ridden a farm horse or brought in the new-laid eggs. And people here make fun of them. I was so lucky being sent to a doctor's family.

Saturday, December 24

Christmas is nearly here. Victoria is acting funny. She has some big secret she is bursting to tell me and she has finally begun to stay away from me in case she lets it slip. I know she is getting a lovely new dress of sprigged muslin with a lace collar. It is to wear to church and parties. She will dance about in it and make the full skirt stand out.

I got Victoria a secondhand copy of *Rose in Bloom* by Louisa May Alcott, partly because Vic's second name is Josephine after Jo March in *Little Women*. I would have bought her her very own copy of that book, but she had taken over the family one and keeps it in her own bookcase. She has *Eight Cousins* there too, and I remember how she loved it. The one I am giving her is the sequel to *Eight Cousins*. It is not as good as the first one, but Victoria will be pleased. She loves reading. I like it but I have always had to work too hard to get the habit of it, the way Vic has. If she is not doing something else, she goes straight to a book and she weeps over the characters and laughs aloud when they do something funny.

Uncle A. measured me up against the door today and put a pencil mark to show how tall I am now. I have grown two whole inches since I came. I was such a little squib in those days. Victoria says she will have to stop calling me Sparrow and call me Heron instead. But I am still my father's Sparrow Wilson inside.

Christmas Day

I got an envelope and inside it was a note saying they have hired Miss Hope to teach me to play the piano! It seems Victoria heard me playing in secret when I thought the family was away. She says she thinks the teacher will really have "high hopes" of me. (They sometimes call her Miss Low Hope because of her struggles with Victoria.) I have my first lesson this very week and Victoria says I am to play so the whole house can hear me. I never guessed she was listening when I just barely touched the keys, picking out tunes so softly.

Victoria gave me a jar of cream to rub on my hands at bedtime so they will be softer and look beautiful on the keys. Jasper snorted rudely, but I think it was very kind. Oh, Mam would be so proud!

Vic was thrilled with her book. She spent all Christmas afternoon rereading it. I had to set the table for dinner without any help from her. Then, just as I finished, Victoria Josephine Cope arrives at the dining room door, red-eyed from crying, to ask if there's anything she could do. I just laughed at her. But inside I was pleased that she loved my present so much.

I won't have as much time for writing in my notebook after Christmas. I will have to practise the piano. But now that Sadie is gone and no longer jeering at my feeling that I belong here, I can be comfortable knowing that I am the Copes' Home Girl. This really is my home. Jasper's too.

I am going to start saving any money that comes my way, so that when I am grown and working as a nurse,

I will be able to make a home for Jasper and buy myself a second-hand piano. I probably will never get enough. But I can try. Mam always said, "Marianna Wilson, you must always dream big dreams if you want to have joy in your life."

Late in the afternoon, when Uncle A. and the three older children went out to pay a Christmas call and Aunt Lily and Rosie were napping, I tried to play the piano right out loud, the way you are supposed to. I didn't pound the keys but I didn't barely touch them the way I had done before. I was playing "O Come, All Ye Faithful" with one finger and it was as easy as anything. Then Aunt Lily's voice, from behind me, said, "Oh, Marianna, I had no idea you could play by ear!" I had no idea I could either.

She showed me some chords and taught me how. And now I can play it with both hands! I said I was sorry if I had wakened her, but she said I hadn't and it was time she began getting our supper of leftovers started. I went to help, of course, but I felt as though my feet had wings.

Merry Christmas, Marianna Wilson, Home Girl and famous pianist!

Chin Mei-ling

An Ocean Apart

The Gold Mountain Diary of Chin Mei-ling
Vancouver, British Columbia
November 1922 – July 1923

BY GILLIAN CHAN

Having done her best to reunite her family — her father in Vancouver, her mother and brother in China — Mei turns her attention to her studies, and the hope that she will one day become a doctor.

An Unexpected Gift

Tuesday, December 21, 1926
Dundas, Ontario

It feels very strange to be writing a diary again, especially as I vowed to leave the last pages empty in my beautiful red diary. Is this a betrayal? No, this is not really a diary, but a little book that Miss MacDonald gave me to write about our trip.

If anyone had told me that I would be in Ontario this Christmas, with Miss MacDonald's family, I would have thought them very foolish. There were many reasons why this could not be: school; my baba would not allow it; we do not have money to waste on a pleasure trip. None mattered in the end. Miss MacDonald made it happen. If I am to study to be a doctor then I have to come to Toronto, as it is not possible to do this in Vancouver. She made the trip happen, the same way she convinced the people in her church here to pay for my studies and even to pay for me to come now so they could meet me. I do not know how she convinced my baba — they are still not comfortable when they talk with each other — but she did, and promised that I would be looked after by her own family. As to school, although I missed the last few days, I probably worked more than those who stayed. Miss MacDonald is a hard taskmaster and as our train travelled across the prairies, I did not have time to admire the snowy scenery. It was all work! Now it is done, and until we go to Toronto for our meeting, I am just a guest. This will be peculiar, as I have never been a guest.

I thought I would be excited but I'm not. This house is too big, with so many rooms and people that I find it very scary. The MacDonalds must be very rich to live in such a place. I had thought that Miss MacDonald's brother would live simply like she does, as he and his wife are missionaries, but she laughed and told me that we are staying with her older brother, the *rich* one, who inherited the family business. The missionary brother has gone back to China.

When I look around my bedroom, it's so pretty that it makes me feel very shabby. The driver who picked us up in Hamilton and drove us to the MacDonalds' house sniffed when he felt how light my valise was. There are other servants here, too — a cook, a cleaner, and a maid. It will feel wrong for me to be waited on by them, when this is what my baba does at home for the Baldwins. I miss him so much already. It does not seem fair that I am sitting idle, while he and the others work so hard. As I sit here enjoying my evening, I think of him finishing his long day at the Baldwins' and still having to work in our restaurant, which is always busy over Christmas.

There were many greetings when we arrived and I found this a trial. Mr. and Mrs. MacDonald are kind, taking me into their home, but they make me nervous. They are very formal and when they speak to me, my words jumble in my mouth. I know I sound foolish. I was glad to escape to my room "to rest and get my bearings," as Miss MacDonald put it. How will I remember everyone's name — there are so many already and more to come. Tomorrow, I will meet the young people of the house — Miss MacDonald's niece and nephew who are returning from Toronto. Over the four years that Miss MacDonald has tutored me, I have heard so much about them that they feel like friends. I hope that they will like me.

My head is drooping and my hand aches. I am out of practice when it comes to writing a diary!

Thursday, December 23, 1926

I am not writing every day. Too many new things are happening all the time. Instead I will write about the main events and Helen and Robert MacDonald (although he says I am to call him Robbie), Miss MacDonald's niece and nephew. I no longer feel so scared and out of place, as they make sure that I am included in all their activities.

Helen is very lively. Since she arrived home from Havergal College, her boarding school, many friends have come to call. Today we walked into Dundas with some of them to shop and take tea. Robbie came too, not willingly, but his mother insisted that teenage girls needed someone older and sensible with them. We went to a big store called Grafton's. It is not as big as Woodward's in Vancouver, but it is very fine. Helen and her friends were like birds darting from counter to counter. I was shocked by how casually they bought things, as if money was not real to them. In fact, they did not even use money, but told the shop assistants to put it on their accounts, which I assume their parents pay. A very sour part of me was jealous. That money would mean much to my baba and me, not for frivolous things like scarves and gewgaws, but to send home to China where it would feed them for many months.

The girls had so many questions for me. I don't think they have spoken to anyone Chinese before. Some questions I did not mind — the ones about school — but others embarrassed me — the ones about my family. My answers were short, but the questions did not stop. Our restaurant fascinated them, and I burned inside when one of Helen's friends said, "How quaint! Perhaps we should take you to one of the Chinese joints in Hamilton so you'll feel at home." I did not answer her but looked away. The others, including Helen, laughed. Robbie spoke then, his voice cutting through the laughter. "That's enough, girls, give May a rest from all the questions." I was very grateful.

After our tea, it was still light and the girls wanted to walk down to see if what they called "the turning basin" was frozen enough to skate on (it was). I have never skated, but I have read about it and think it might be fun. Helen whispered that she had old skates that would fit me. I think it was her way of apologizing for laughing earlier.

As we walked, I stayed back from the girls a little. I had had my fill of questions. Robbie slowed his pace and walked with me, talking at little. He asked questions, too, but these I did not mind so much because they were to do with my work with his aunt and my plans for medical school. He is very quiet in his manner, not like Ivor at home who is always loud and full of his own opinions. I could talk to Robbie and ask questions too. He is in his first year at the University of Toronto. This made me happy because I will know someone when I come in two years time, but when I said this, he sighed and said, "For a little while, perhaps." His face got very downcast and he told me that although he would like to study and be a minister like his uncle, his father will not allow it. Robbie is expected to take over the family business. I was surprised. I thought that when you were rich, you had no problems and life was always easy.

Friday, December 24, 1926

It is very late and I am tired and overwhelmed. Although today was meant to be devoted to a party, it has also been an important day for me because I have learned what I must face in the future.

I realize now how rich and important Miss MacDonald's older brother must be. There was a huge open house today. I have never seen so much food. Extra servants were hired to help. So many people came that I lost count of them all.

I did not know how I should dress, so I put on my best clothes, the ones I have been saving to meet the people at the university: the dark serge skirt and the new white blouse that Mrs. Lee, at home, helped me make. She has been teaching me to sew when she makes clothes for her children. I had not worn them before and felt very smart.

Helen knocked on my door when it was time to go down. I do not think I am a vain girl, but my heart sank when her face lost her smile the moment she saw me.

"Don't you have any party clothes, May?" she asked.

I shook my head.

"I'll lend you some," Helen said, "we're about the same size. It will be fun to dress you up." Grabbing my hand she pulled me toward her room.

I did not intend to be rude, but perhaps it was the way she spoke, making me sound like a plaything, a doll, to be dressed. I freed my hand from hers, saying that these clothes were my best ones and I wanted to wear them.

Helen shrugged and said, "Suit yourself. I was only trying to help." She walked toward the stairs without once looking back to see if I was following her.

Downstairs, I regretted my stubbornness. I looked like a crow in a field of peacocks. Only the men and boys wore dark suits; the girls and women wore every colour there was. Even Miss MacDonald wore a lilac dress, one that was beautiful even if it looked old-fashioned. Helen had found a group of her friends. I think she was talking about me, since she kept glancing in my direction. People were staring and I felt very self-conscious. I moved toward Miss MacDonald, keeping my eyes down.

I was almost there when a large, freckled hand pushed a glass toward me. It very nearly hit my face. I stopped, shocked, and looked up. The glass was thrust forward again. An elderly lady was staring at me. "Girl, go and get me more punch," she ordered. I knew that tone of voice. I heard it in our restaurant when Canadians ordered Wong Bak around. I heard it once when I was waiting for my baba and Mrs. Baldwin was giving him his orders for the next day. It is a tone that expects to be obeyed without question. I shrivelled inside, but reached for the glass.

Another hand got there before mine. Robbie stood beside me, a tight, polite smile on his face. His voice broke the silence that had overtaken the room. "Mrs. Overfield, all our servers seem to be busy at the moment, let me get you the punch." He linked his other arm through mine. "Perhaps, May, you would like to come with me and get some punch, too, then I will introduce you to *some of our other guests.*"

Conversation swelled up again. I was glad. I wanted the noise to blot everything else out. Robbie found a server and told her to fill the glass and take it back to Mrs. Overfield. He started to apologize for her behaviour, but I stopped him. It was not his fault. When he repeated his offer to introduce me to others, I did not refuse, but I doubted that I would recall the people I met. That old woman's voice kept ringing in my head. It still is, even now, hours later.

Since I have been here I've learned how I am seen because I am Chinese. I thought it might be different in Ontario, but it isn't, not really. We are servants, and if we are not, then we are exotic oddities to be questioned and commented upon. Sometimes all I want is just to be Mei-ling, a girl with hopes and dreams like any other.

Christmas Day

I fought away my gloom of yesterday, eager to be part of my first ever Christmas celebrations. They were not fun! Church, church and more church! Mr. MacDonald and poor Robbie went three times! The ladies only went twice: in the morning and for an evening service. I have come to like church, although it pains my baba, as he feels it takes me away from him, but this was too much for me! Between the morning and evening service, we had a big, formal meal. Helen and Robbie sat at one end of the table with me, and I was surprised by how little their parents talk to them. Miss MacDonald tried to include them and me in the conversation, but her brother quickly steered it back to his business. After dinner, we retired to the drawing room, where there were presents to be opened. I thought I should go to my room, as this was a family time. I was shamed that I had no gifts for my hosts. Miss MacDonald took my hand and told me that none was expected from me, just as none was expected from her, since she earned so little. My embarrassment grew when there was a present for me, a large present: a beautiful winter coat with a fur collar. Mr. MacDonald said that it was practical and I would need it for Ontario winters when I come to university. I could not speak, as I was so overwhelmed, and my eyes filled with tears.

The coat is lying beside me as I write. I keep touching it. I have never owned anything so beautiful and so expensive. Baba will not like this gift. He hates that he cannot give me much. He does not realize how much he does give me though: his companionship, his love and the strength to hold onto our dream of being a family once more.

Sunday, December 26, 1926

I have had the most wonderful day. There was a skating party this afternoon. It seemed like all the young people of Dundas were at the turning basin. There were some older people, but not many. Miss MacDonald came, but did not skate. Helen was true to her words, finding skates for me. They worked once I stuffed some paper in the toes. I wore my new coat, and it was very warm; the fur collar snuggled around my throat.

A tiny part of me worried that I would be the object of much staring, but I was given no chance to dwell on this. Robbie made sure of that. He was like a guardian angel, patient and putting up with my wobbliness. At first he skated backwards, holding both my hands so that I would not fall. As I got braver and could manage to glide rather than do tottering little steps, he linked his arm through mine, and in the end, we could go round and round like other people. We talked a lot. He is very kind, and when I am with him I can forget that people are looking at me, that I am thought unusual. I am just myself, someone whom he finds interesting, which makes me very happy.

Helen skated with her friends, cheering my progress every time she whizzed by. My face went red when she said that Robbie and I looked like a courting couple. Robbie told me to ignore her, but I noticed that while most people skated alone, there were some who had paired off.

It was dark when we got back. Helen and Robbie's

parents were in the hallway waiting for the car to take them to a dinner party. Miss MacDonald had elected to stay with "the young people." I liked that, but I did not like Helen repeating her comment that Robbie and I had looked like a courting couple.

Robbie did not either, as his voice was sharp when he said, "Oh, grow up, Helen! Don't be such an idiot."

Mr. MacDonald gave Robbie a very hard look and told him not to be so rude to his sister.

Helen is foolish. She makes something out of nothing.

Monday, December 27, 1926

Today has been strange. It is our last day here before we leave for our meeting in Toronto tomorrow.

Last night Helen had asked Robbie if he would take us to Hamilton to see a film called *Beau Geste* that she says is "all the rage." He agreed.

This morning, however, there was no sign of him. Helen had gone to the house of a friend, so it was not until she returned for lunch that she asked where he was. Her mother said that Robbie had had to go to Toronto on some errands for their father and would be staying there for a few days.

Helen pouted and whined that Robbie had promised to take us to the cinema and that he had said nothing about errands. Her mother's face became very stern and she told Helen to stop, that the errands had come up suddenly, and that she was spoiled to make such a fuss. Helen did stop, but she sulked through the whole meal.

I was not sad about not seeing the film, but I was sad that I would not have a chance to talk more with Robbie and to say goodbye properly.

After lunch I went with Miss MacDonald to visit some of her friends. They were very kind to me, and did not ask me too many questions about myself, thank goodness! Miss MacDonald seemed quiet and a little out of sorts. I do hope that she is not sickening for something. Helen had told me that there have been cases of Scarlet Fever in Dundas.

Things are not well in this house, and I do not know why. Helen was bored before dinner so she taught me to play cribbage, a card game that I liked a lot. We were playing in the drawing room next to Mr. MacDonald's study. We could hear raised voices coming from there. It sounded like Miss MacDonald and Helen's father. Helen and I looked at each other. She shrugged as if to say that she did not know what is was about.

Dinner was very quiet. The only ones who talked at all were Helen and I.

Tuesday, December 28, 1926

I am writing this in our compartment on the train. It has been a day of sadness and joy, and perhaps writing things down will help me be clear about how I feel.

Miss MacDonald was tight-lipped this morning when we left for Toronto. Only Mrs. MacDonald and Helen were there to see us off. Miss MacDonald sniffed and made a comment that her brother never could face up to unpleasantness.

"Oh, Agnes, he's just doing what he thinks best," was Mrs. MacDonald's reply.

It was obvious that Miss MacDonald and her brother had fallen out over something. When we were finally on the train she explained what it was, and I was mortified.

Mr. MacDonald had taken Helen's joking words to heart and had sent Robbie away because he did not want him forming "unsuitable attachments." That is me. I am the unsuitable attachment!

My face must have shown my feelings because Miss MacDonald explained further, telling me that her brother had more on his mind than just the friendship that had grown up between me and Robbie. I interrupted her to tell her that Helen was wrong and it was truly only a friendship! She patted my hand and said she knew that, but her brother worried that Robbie did not want to take over the family business. He feared that seeing someone like me who was willing to fight against the odds to study and fulfill a dream might give Robbie ideas. This was what she had argued with her brother about last night. She said that Robbie should do what he wanted, not be forced into something he might come to hate. She sighed, saying that she thought her brother would not have been so blinkered in this thoughts.

I was very confused and sad that I should be the cause of such trouble. I do like Robbie a great deal, but I never dreamed that people would think badly of that.

Miss MacDonald peered anxiously at me and asked if I could put this out of my mind when we visited the people at the Missionary Society, as it was important that I make a good impression and convince them of my seriousness and ability. I think she was a little surprised at how quickly and firmly I said that I could.

I hope it is not boastful to say that the meeting went well. Three people talked to us, and I was able to answer all their questions. I did blush when Miss MacDonald talked about me and told them how dedicated I was. I went even more red when she read aloud a letter from my high school principal. They smiled at this, and one said, "Clever, but modest, too!"

Once we were out of the interview room, Miss MacDonald hugged me and whispered, "May, I am so proud of you!"

We had to go straight to Union Station to catch our train for the long journey to Vancouver. Miss MacDonald was trying to hail a taxicab when I heard footsteps pounding toward us. When I turned to see what was happening, I saw Robbie. His face was red and he was panting slightly.

"I didn't think I would catch you in time," he said. "My father had arranged all sorts of appointments with his suppliers for me today, but I'll miss the last one if I have to, and face the consequences later."

My heart filled with joy when he said that he could not let me go without saying goodbye and that he would keep in touch through his aunt.

She smiled at that. I was a little shocked when she laughed and said that she had always been good at sneaking things around her brother!

Robbie put out his hand as if to shake mine, but then held on to my hand as he said, "I will help you, May, when you come here. You can count on that!"

My eyes felt prickly with tears, but I did not cry. Instead I smiled and thanked him.

After the sadness of today, now there is joy, too, knowing that I will not be alone when I am so far from home.

Robbie will be a good friend to have. Only a friend, though. I can allow nothing to stop me from becoming a doctor. It is not something I just dream of doing. It is something I *must* do. So much depends upon it.

Arabella Stevenson

A Rebel's Daughter

The 1837 Diary of Arabella Stevenson
Toronto, Upper Canada
December 1837 — October 1838

BY JANET LUNN

Arabella doesn't yet own a diary. In fact, she doesn't even like the idea of one. But in her long letter to her friend Jane about a memorable Christmas Day in 1836 — almost a year before the turmoil of the coming rebellion — we see glimmers of the devoted diarist that Arabella will one day become.

Stevenson House
Toronto, Upper Canada
26 December, 1836

Dear Jane,

I am *so* happy that you are finally out of danger. Almost half the girls in school have the measles. Sophie Allwood is said to be dreadfully ill. I wish I could come to see you but, of course, I cannot. So I am sending you this bit of Christmas cake and a few of the sweetmeats from the Bons Bons Miss St. Clair brought on Christmas Day. (I filched them from the sideboard in the dining room before Peggy had a chance to clear after Christmas dinner.) Also I absolutely must tell you about our amazing Christmas. You will be so entertained by the events of Christmas Day *chez* Stevenson that you will forget all about your horrid spots.

Christmas Day began in the usual fashion. Our house was *beautiful.* I helped put the cedar garland on the balusters and stair railing, and pine boughs and cones and lovely white candles on all the mantels (and I made certain to have some in my bedroom). We exchanged gifts after breakfast (it was ham and baked eggs and absolutely perfect cinnamon rolls). I think Papa liked the penwipe I made for him, Charlie said he liked his scarf and I hope Mama liked her handkerchief as I had laboured over it mightily. Papa gave me a copy of *The Pilgrim's Progress*, Mama gave me a handkerchief that was much finer than the one I gave her (I think it came from France) and Charlie gave me a box of sugar fruits (his favourites, he has already eaten half of them). We were all quite jolly.

We went to church in the morning, all dressed in our Christmas best. (Jane, I had such a beautiful new deep-green velvet dress with lace on the collar — but I will tell you more about that later!) Dr. Strachan preached in his usual Scottish voice about charity but that was bearable because we sang "For Unto Us a Child is Born" and "Adeste Fideles." I do love the singing. Then we came home to our usual quiet Christmas dinner which, oh woe, always includes Miss St. Clair. (Jane, do you not think headmistresses ought not be invited to Christmas dinner? Or any other dinner?) Mama says that Miss St. C. is, "after all, an English gentlewoman without friend or relation on this side of the ocean," and you know how

Mama is about everything that is English! She talks sometimes as though *she* had not a friend or relation on this side of the ocean. It is true, of course, she does *not* have her mama and papa here.

Well, the usualness was gone the absolute instant we arrived inside our house. There in the drawing room were Gran and Granddad and Great-Aunt Laura Henry (she is Gran's sister and she lives with them). Neighbours from down the road from their farm decided to hire a carriage to come to Toronto for their granddaughter's wedding, and they thought Gran and Graddad might like to come along and surprise us with a visit. Well they *did* surprise us. We stared at them as though they had suddenly appeared from nowhere, as people do in fairy tales.

Then Gran jumped up from her chair. Granddad stood. Mama gave a little shriek. Then she made her face smile. (I expect because Miss St. C. was there. My mother is as good as a pantomime, she can make her face do whatever she wishes.)

I was so glad to see Gran and Granddad. We hugged and hugged and kissed and kissed and then we did it all over again. Jane, you would like Gran and Granddad exceedingly, I know you would. My granddad has a bushy black beard and he looks as fierce as a bear but he is not fierce, he is jolly and makes jokes all the time. He has a loud voice and an even louder laugh. Gran is forever saying, "Now Josiah, there are those among us who do not find farmyard animals as amusing as you do." She is certainly right. Mama does not find his stories one bit amusing.

Papa and Charlie were greeting Gran and Granddad and Great-Aunt L. H. Mama was trying to introduce Miss St. C. to them. (I do not think she cared to do this as she thinks Gran and Granddad and Great-Aunt L. H. are not fine enough for her.) Peggy was trying to take our cloaks and bonnets. It was what Gran calls "a real stirabout." Then there was a knock on the door.

You will never guess who it was. Never. It was Charlie's friend, horrid Jesse Harvard. The measles have struck the Harvard family. Two of their maids are ill with them and so is Elizabeth (I told you that half the school has them). J. was sent with his small sister Charlotte to their Aunt Harvard. You know what an old tartar she is! (Remember when she marched into school in a rage at Elizabeth because E. had let her cat into the muddy garden?) So, when we were coming out of church, J. was complaining to Charlie and C. invited him for Christmas dinner.

As you can imagine, I did not find *this* one bit amusing. I think Mama would have had one of her fits right then and there but for Miss St. C. (Can you believe that I was actually happy that Miss St. C. was here?) Mama welcomed J. with a pretty smile, then she hissed into my ear that I was to go right down to the kitchen and tell Sophie that there would be four more places at the dinner table.

Peggy has come to say that dinner is served. I will have to finish this later.

Here I am, back from dinner. It was stewed beef with more potatoes and carrots than beef in it but there was lovely sugar pie for afterwards.

Back to my story. Off I went down to the kitchen. Sophie was already busy multiplying the loaves and fishes. She said, "Now Miss Belle, tell your ma not to fret. That roast of beef is big enough to go around twice over for a dozen people." Then she told me that Gran had brought two hens and four minced pies and enough green tomato pickle to make Papa happy for a year.

I went back upstairs just in time to see three more people come through the front doorway, a man and a woman and a boy. Complete strangers — and they had *baggage*. I was aching to know who they were but I knew Mama would send me, so down to the kitchen I went. Sophie just said, "Don't bother me again until you got the final count." I decided right then that nothing in the world could ever happen that would upset Sophie.

It turned out that the people in the hall were called Rubidge. They are Horatio Rubidge, Maria Rubidge and their son Jasper Rubidge, who is seven years old. They are some sort of cousins to Mama and they have come from England and have been making their way from Montreal over this past month. They mean to homestead in the backwoods, miles and miles north of the farm country where Gran and Granddad live. They know no one else in Toronto so they came to us. Not that they know us but they had our direction (on a bit of smudged paper) from a cousin who has been writing letters to Mama.

What a mess (a Sophie word) of people we were. I wished to know all about these English cousins and, even more, I wished to visit with my gran and granddad but Mama told me that I was to help Peggy settle the cousins in the guest room and then entertain Jasper until dinner. Jane, do you not think this was truly unfair? Jasper is a boy. Mama should have asked Charlie and that wretched Jesse Harvard to entertain him but, of course, those boys had disappeared. I was stuck with Jasper.

You cannot believe what a dreadful boy he is. The only boy I have ever really known is Charlie and you know how dreadful *he* can be! Well this boy is totally, completely, unbelievably more dreadful! He is small and thin and straw-haired and so quiet you scarcely notice he is about but he is quick and sly — and *mean*. He invents the most astonishing devilment. I had to lock my poor little Dolly in my bedroom for fear he meant to murder her (I put the key on a string about my neck). She got out the first time when I went to hide my china-headed dolls away but, after Jasper threw her down the dumbwaiter the *second* time, she was very happy to stay in my bedroom.

Jasper's father and mother do absolutely nothing to stop the devilment. Actually I doubt they are able. They are the feeblest human beings you can possibly imagine. They look exactly alike. Exactly! They are both as skinny as Patty's old orange cat and Mr. R. has thin hair that same faded orange colour. Mrs. R. has mouse-grey hair (that is the only difference). She speaks in such a soft voice one must strain to hear even half what she says and Mr. R. giggles after every second word. I cannot imagine how they will manage out in the bush. They are not real cousins. Mrs. R. is cousin to the cousin who corresponds with Mama. (I do not suppose you find that a bit interesting, but I do like to have things properly sorted out.)

Peggy took Mr. and Mrs. R. upstairs and I was left to entertain Jasper. I had not the least notion how I was to do so. (I was wishing you were here because you always have such good ideas.) I asked him if he liked books. He did not. I asked if he liked music. He did not. (I was glad about that. I might have had to play the Mozart song we have been learning. What a notion!)

I was trying my best to think of what to do when he darted into the dining room. He went straight to the table which was set for dinner and began to upend everything on it. He had just got nicely started (with me scurrying along behind) when Peggy came in to set the new places. Our maid is not patient with children (as you know). She lunged at him, grabbed him around his middle and pulled his hand from one of the tall silver candlesticks. He wriggled loose. He spied Miss St. C.'s Bons Bons on the sideboard. I told you he was quick. Peggy was quicker. She took him by the arm and marched him smartly out of the dining room (otherwise you would not have the sweetmeats I sent).

That was when he grabbed my poor cat by her tail and threw her down the dumbwaiter the first time. While I was below stairs, rescuing Dolly, Jasper was upstairs in the nursery overturning everything. I found him there after I had put Dolly in my bedroom. I wrested my dolls from his clutches and took them to keep Dolly company (which is when she ran out). While I was doing that, Jasper disappeared again.

Jane, I confess that I did not follow him. I stole back into the drawing room and stood just inside the door where Mama could not see me. Granddad saw me and so did Papa. They both smiled and Granddad winked.

Mama was sitting in one of the chairs near the fire asking Mrs. Rubidge for news from England. Miss St. C. was sitting in the opposite chair, listening as though she knew Mama's relatives as well as Mama does. Great-Aunt L. H., with her bonnet still on her head, was drooping on the loveseat. Great-Aunt L. H. droops like a wilted rose.

Papa and Granddad were standing by the drinks table laughing about something I could not hear and Gran was across the room, smiling happily at both of them — my gran is so — so — oh, I cannot think of just the word for Gran but she makes everything feel *absolutely right* in the whole, entire world.

Another interruption. This time it was Dolly jumping into my lap. I all but turned over the ink bottle. Now she has settled down to purr. (She is a *very* quiet cat today.)

Back to Christmas Day. Papa began to pass around the wine and the cordial. That was when Jasper threw Dolly down the dumbwaiter the second time. She landed with a thunderous crash on the dishes Sophie had put there to send upstairs, and she let out a *horrifical* screech. Mama screamed. Mrs. R. moaned. We all raced out into the hall to see what had happened. Charlie and Jesse came thumping down the stairs from Charlie's room. Dolly flew by up the stairs. I ran after her.

I found her scratching at my door. Her eyes were wild and her fur was standing straight up and she was covered with something *really* sticky. My poor Dolly! I picked her up and carried her into my bedroom. She jumped out of my arms and was under my bed in a flash. All I could see was her tail thrashing like fury. I had to leave her there to recover from her terrrible ordeal. (This was when I locked my door.)

It was mashed, sugared turnip all over Dolly — and all over me and my new green velvet dress. I discovered what it was when I went down to the kitchen to look for Jasper. He was not there. Charlie and Jesse were and Sophie was. Sophie was scraping mashed, sugared turnip and bits of Mama's best china serving bowl from the dumbwaiter. Jane, I was wrong to think that nothing could truly upset Sophie. Her face was as red as a tomato and she sent us all from the kitchen with just one word, "GO."

Up on the first floor, everyone was on the way back into the drawing room. I could not see either Mr. or Mrs. R.'s face but, from the back, they both looked as though they were trying to shrink.

Mama was *very* angry. She only said to me that I was to find THE BOY "at once," but her jaw was tight shut and there was fire in her eyes.

I looked in the dining room — and under the table. He was not there. I looked in the pantry. He was not there. I knew he was not in the drawing room so I looked in Papa's study. He was not there. I looked in the hidey place but he had not discovered that. I went upstairs and looked in Charlie's room. C. and J. were there but not THE BOY and you can be sure that *they* were not concealing him. He was not in Papa's room nor in Mama's. (Not even THE BOY could be bold enough to invade Mama's sanctuary.) I was on my way down the stairs, trying to think where to look next, when I heard Sophie say, very slowly, "Get – yourself – out – of – there. *This* minute."

She was not precisely shouting but I am sure that one could hear her everywhere in the house and possibly outside — and, possibly, all the way to Yonge Street. I was through the dining room and into the pantry (just ahead of the crowd) in time to see THE BOY crawl out of the dumbwaiter and into the pantry. When he saw us all coming towards him, he dropped down and tried to crawl past us but you know how big Sophie is. She put one hand around his skinny arm and held fast. Mrs. R. began to cry. No one said a word until, finally, Granddad said, "Well, youngster, how about sitting with me for a while?"

THE BOY said nothing. Granddad laughed. He put his arm so tightly around him that THE BOY *had* to go into the drawing room and sit beside Granddad in his chair.

All this time Mr. R. did nothing and said nothing. Nothing at all. Mrs. R. went on weeping into her handkerchief. I went to my room to wash my hands and arms and my face and change into my old red wool dress. Alas and alack, I do not believe the green velvet will outlive the turnip. I was not (I am not) in charity with THE BOY!

Do you think this is the end of my Christmas tale? Well, it is not.

Mama was trying very hard to get Miss St. C. and Mr. and Mrs. R. to talk about England. In his big voice, Granddad was telling THE BOY about his cows. THE BOY sat absolutely still, looking as though he had never in his life thought about getting up to mischief. He looked as you might imagine an angel — except that his blue tunic was streaked with dirt (perhaps it was mashed, sugared turnip) and his white collar was quite black. I sat down beside Gran but I did not feel as I usually do with her because everything was so discombobricated. (Mama hates it when I use slang but I love that word.)

Finally Peggy announced dinner. Papa grandly offered his arm to Miss St. C., to lead her into dinner. Granddad offered his arm to Mama, Mr. R. offered his to Great-Aunt L. H. Charlie (after Mama nudged him) did the same for Gran, and Jesse started after me with his arm but Mama shoved him at Mrs. R. I had to follow after with THE BOY (not that I wanted to take J. H.'s arm).

Oh, Jane, I had to leave you again. Charlie came charging into my room because he was sure I would know where his muffler is. I do not — THE BOY likely took a fancy to it.

Back to my story. The table had our best linen cloth on it and Mama's best china. The ring of cedar around the tall silver candlesticks in the centre looked very pretty and the candles shone brightly on the small crystal dishes with the green and red and yellow pickles and relishes. Except that I had to sit next to THE BOY, I quite liked having so many people at dinner.

In came Peggy with the soup — it was almond soup, Mama's favourite (not mine). Then, of course, she brought in the roast beef, then the roasted chickens, the bread sauce, the beaten potatoes, the boiled carrots, the creamed onion, and the parsnip pudding (but no mashed, sugared turnip).

I was watching him very carefully and THE BOY did not make a single bit of trouble all through dinner. He was too busy eating. (A prodigious amount — I could scarcely believe it when he took a fifth piece of chicken from the platter Peggy passed him — and he did not complain about the soup.) C. and J. were every bit as busy at their dinners. The adults all talked — about what Christmas was like in England in the manor house where Mama lived when she was a girl, what it was like for Gran and Granddad when their families were pioneers here in Upper Canada when it was entirely wilderness. It was really nice.

Then Peggy cleared the table and it was Christmas pudding time. Peggy was passing it around on Mama's best blue serving plate. I was watching her as she came towards our end of the table (I love Christmas pudding and I feared there would be only a scant portion left by the time it reached me) so I was almost facing THE BOY. I wish I had been watching him more closely because, when I chanced to look at his face for one instant, his face looked exactly like the picture of Rumpelstiltskin in your fairy-tale book. I looked down and saw his hand go under his tunic. Then the tail of a *rat* dropped below the hem. I told you THE BOY was quick. He had the rat out from under his tunic and onto the pudding plate before I could make one sound.

For a second no one else did, either. Then Peggy screamed and threw the plate of pudding and rat onto the table. The rat rolled off onto the tablecloth. (Did I tell you it was a *dead* rat?) Mama went white. Miss St. C. screamed and leapt to her feet. Great-Aunt L. H. said, "Oh, my," and fainted. Mrs. R. began to cry again. Granddad reached over and put the rat back on the pudding plate. Papa stood up and picked up the plate and carried it into the pantry (Peggy had run off). C. and J. started laughing so hard I thought they would fall off their chairs. Mr. R. went right on eating his pudding. I just sat and stared. I could *not* believe what had happened.

Do you think *this* is the end of my Christmas tale? It is not. There is one more bit.

While all this excitement was happening, THE BOY said nothing. He did nothing, either. I was thinking that, if I were to look at him and he was looking pleased with himself, I might strike him. I did look at him but he was not looking pleased with himself. His pale face had gone as white as skimmed milk. One second later he leaned forward and threw up all over the table.

That was the end of our Christmas day but not the *absolute* end of the story. Mrs. R. took THE BOY upstairs. Everyone else had tea in the drawing room and then the Toronto visitors went home.

The Rubidge family will be here for at least a fortnight but *I* will not. Charlie and I are to go home with Gran and Granddad and Great-Aunt L. H.

THE BOY has the measles.

I hope you are feeling entirely well very soon.

Affectionately,
your friend Arabella

Mary Macdonald

With Nothing But Our Courage

The Loyalist Diary of Mary Macdonald
Jamestown, Québec

October 1783 – November 1784

BY KARLEEN BRADFORD

*Run out of Albany for being loyal to the British crown,
Mary and her family endured a long, difficult trek north
to Québec. Even here, with the conflicts of the
Revolutionary War behind them, they are faced with
the struggle of clearing the land given to each Loyalist,
and building their homes in the rough wilderness
of a new land.*

The Word for Home

December 25th, 1784
Johnstown, Quebec

I haven't had much time for journaling, with Grannie handing me a broom or a pail every time she spots me with nothing in my hands. There's no escaping her determination that every corner and nook of this small cabin will be swept as clean as a whistle before the new year comes in. And just a week to go before Hogmanay.

Today's Christmas Day — a day of rest for some of our neighbours, and a day for us Scots to pray and give thanks. And we have so much to give thanks for. If we're careful, we'll have food enough for the winter, and we are snug in our own little cabin, hewed out of the woods with our own hands. (Father taught me that word. I love it. Isn't it fortunate that Father is a schoolmaster?) We all hewed. Mother, Father, Angus and me. Though he is too young to wield an axe, Jamie did his share by piling up the branches. Oh, and

Duncan hewed, too, of course. He's almost family now and he helped as much as anybody else. Perhaps even more. Father says he's a good worker and I certainly agree.

I am so glad Angus brought Duncan back from the war with him. And the other day when he took his muddy boots off I saw he was wearing the socks I knitted for him! In fact, he gave me a small, private grin and made certain that I noticed. He seems much happier lately. Ever since he told me that he had broken with his family to fight with the British against the American Rebels, I have felt so sorry for him. But it makes for a very warm feeling inside me to know that he thought me special enough to tell. None of the rest of our family, aside from Angus, knows his secret.

I am looking at my hands right now and feeling proud of every callus and rough spot. Chopping down trees was very satisfying. And watching the beans grow in the garden that Mother and I scrabbled in amongst the stumps — even though they were the only seeds that we could plant because it was so late by the time we got a small garden cleared — was so gratifying. Father and his Indian friends have caught so many fish that we have a whole barrel salted down and, thanks to Angus and Duncan's good shooting, their bear will supply us with meat until spring. (I was *so* tired of salt pork after having no other meat for so many months after we left Albany. Mother kept saying we were fortunate to have it, but I notice she avoids it like the plague now too.)

Our cabin is snug and warm; the fire is blazing. Even though Mittens is getting to be a big cat she is curled up on the hearth in her favourite spot, right between Laddie's paws. Laddie is snoring mightily, his nose twitching and his paws scrabbling a bit, which is making Mittens curious. Any moment now I'm sure she'll be batting at them. She's not too grown-up for that. I wonder what Laddie is dreaming of? I wonder if he ever remembers the home he lost when he was a puppy? Jamie loves him beyond reason and I love him too. Especially when he isn't too smelly.

We won't be celebrating Christmas other than with prayers, of course, but I remember how it was last year when we were at Machiche, how kind Mrs. Livingstone was, and what a feast she gave us on Christmas Day. I can still smell that goose.

Grannie is glaring at me right now and waving a broom. I'd better put this journal away and get to work. I'll write more when I have time. I can't thank Father enough for giving me this new journal for my fourteenth birthday last week. I'd filled every page of my old one and I didn't know what I would do. Writing in it for the past year after we were driven out of Albany by the Rebels has helped me so much, I couldn't imagine how I was going to carry on without it. But Father made me up a new one himself from the supplies he got for the school.

I didn't realize that he knew how much having a journal to pour my thoughts into means to me. I should have, though. Father and I have always had a special understanding.

Uh-oh, Grannie is bustling over and she looks fit to be tied.

Away with you, journal!

Later

What a lovely day it turned out to be. Angus and Duncan came by from their own shanties and brought raccoon skins. Though they're grateful the British gave them land of their own in return for their loyalty, those shanties are far less comfortable than our own snug cabin, and they do seem to visit as often as they can.

Jamie is delighted that Angus remembered his promise to make him a raccoon hat, and I will have warm mittens. Then Mr. Murchison turned up early this afternoon and we were able to have prayers with him and we sang all my favourite hymns. Grannie was so pleased. She has not stopped smiling since. Mr. Murchison is staying the night and she filled him so full of squirrel stew for supper that I thought he would burst. He will leave early tomorrow morning, however, as he wishes to go on to the Rosses' and the weather looks threatening. I told him I could smell snow, and my nose is never wrong.

I have written a note that he has promised to give to Hannah. I haven't seen her for over a month.

Time to blow out my candle and snuggle down beneath my quilt now. Jamie is sound asleep and snuffling a bit. He sounds like a puppy.

December 27th, 1784

My nose is never wrong. It is snowing heavily outside. Chores must be done anyway, so I will have to leave my warm nest of a bed and brave the cold. The water in the basin beside me is frozen solid. Oh, how I do not want to get up! But get up I must, and get Jamie up too. The animals must be fed and Bess the Second milked.

Take a deep breath. Here goes!

Later

Oh, dear, what a dreadful thing has happened! I dug Jamie out of bed and chivvied him into his warmest clothes and out we went into the blizzard.

Laddie, of course, was right at our heels. We fed the chickens and the geese, milked Bess, made certain the lambs — sheep now, really — had fodder, and slopped the pig. All done at top speed because I was most dreadfully cold and anxious for the bowl of hot porridge that I knew would be waiting for me.

Then, just as we were making our way back from the shed to our cabin, there was a most tremendous clap of thunder! I have never heard thunder before with snow! Before we could grab hold of him, Laddie lit out for the bush. Jamie called and called and would have gone barging through the snow after the dog if I hadn't wrapped my arms around him and held him back. I had to drag him to the cabin. It was snowing so hard by then that I could barely see our way back and I knew we had to take shelter. There was no question of going after Laddie. But now Jamie is huddled by the fire, crying, and will not eat a bite. I couldn't force even a swallow of porridge down either.

There's nothing we can do but hope the fool dog will find his way back.

December 28th, 1784

Still snowing. Laddie still not back. The wind is howling around the cabin like a thousand lost souls in torment. Despite the care we took in chinking between the logs, drafts whistle in up here in the loft. My candle flame is flickering so much that I am afraid it will blow out. Jamie is inconsolable.

December 29th, 1784

Now I do have a story to tell.

I awoke this morning and lay for a moment wondering what was different. Something was missing. And then I realized that the wind had stopped. I leaped out of bed and climbed down the ladder, ignoring the cold completely. I couldn't see anything through the greased paper that Mother had covered the windows with, so I lifted the latch and pulled the door open. What a sight! Snow everywhere, glistening and sparkling in the early morning sun. It made a wall halfway up the doorway. But it had stopped falling. There was such a dead silence outside. I couldn't hear a thing except the occasional soft plop of a blob of snow falling off the tree that we left standing beside the cabin to give us shade in the summer. I just drank in the clear, crisp air.

And then Grannie let out a holler.

"What do you think you're doing?" she cried, heading for me with fire in her eyes and a switch in her hand, but I nipped back up the ladder before she could reach me.

The moment Jamie realized that it had stopped snowing, he was determined to go after Laddie, but Mother would have none of it.

"The dog will find his own way home," she said. "I won't have you traipsing off in the woods."

Jamie stuck out his lip and looked sullen. Then Father gave him a hug.

"I'm off to cut wood and see how Angus and Duncan have fared," he said. "I'll keep a lookout for your dog. Don't worry."

But there was no reasoning with Jamie. We went out to do our chores and feed the animals. I stayed back to gather up the slop pail and when I came out of the shed there was no sign of him. Fresh tracks led off into the woods. My heart just sank like a stone. I ploughed through the snow back to the cabin as fast as I could.

"Jamie's gone off to look for Laddie," I gasped as soon as I got in the door. "I have to go after him!"

"You'll do no such thing," Mother said, but I'm just as stubborn as Jamie. Father was long gone, and we couldn't let Jamie wander around in the woods by himself. Mother has not been too well because of the baby she expects in the spring and she couldn't go. Grannie of course is much too old. I kept on and on at Mother until finally she gave in. I assured her I'd follow Jamie's tracks and catch up to him quickly, then make him turn back and we'd follow our tracks home. "We'll be fine," I said. And I really believed we would.

But I hadn't reckoned with the wolves.

I have to stop now. My candle is guttering out and I cannot write more. I will finish my story tomorrow.

December 30th, 1784

The wolves. I have never been so frightened in my life. Not even when we heard that bear when we were picking blueberries last summer. Here's what happened:

I caught up to Jamie easily, but of course he would not turn around. I had to trail him for the longest time, pleading and then threatening him. Finally I laid hands on him and was about to force him to turn back when I caught sight of something moving in the woods beside us. Something grey. I let go of Jamie and hissed at him to stop walking and be quiet. I must have sounded serious because for once in his life he obeyed me.

I stared into the woods and suddenly realized that eyes were staring back at me. Yellow eyes. A lot of them. And then I realized that a pack of wolves was standing in the trees, staring at us. There must have been about five or six of them.

"Wolves!" I whispered, and pointed.

Jamie turned as pale as the snow.

"What are we going to do?" he whispered back.

For a moment I couldn't think. I just froze in place.

"Don't look at them," I said. Hadn't Angus told me not to look a wild beast in the eyes if I ever came across one? "Let's just start walking slowly back."

I took his hand and we began to retrace our steps. I wouldn't look straight at the wolves, but to my horror I could see that they were keeping pace with us. I could see their forms slinking in and out of the trees beside us. My heart was pounding so hard I was certain they could hear it, but I had to make myself stay calm so as not to frighten Jamie.

I told him as quietly as I could that it would be all right, willing my voice not to tremble. But I didn't believe myself, and Jamie didn't either.

I don't know how long we fought our way back through the snow. We could follow the path we had made coming out, but even so, it seemed to be taking so much longer to go back.

The wolves never made a noise and that made it even more frightening. They just stalked us. Then I realized we were coming to the clearing we had made around our cabin. What would the wolves do then? We would be completely exposed to them and it was too far to the cabin to run for it. The wolves seemed to sense our fear and began to close in. I stopped in my tracks and clutched Jamie to me, not even trying to pretend that I wasn't terrified anymore.

The wolves spread out and began to encircle us. I picked up a branch and held it high, but I knew it would not be of any use.

And then — oh, thanks be to the mercy of God — and then I heard a shot ring out. One wolf fell dead even as he was about to spring, and the rest disappeared back into the woods. I looked up and there stood one of the Indians that Father had befriended. The younger one. The one who looked to be about the same age as Angus. He just nodded to me and motioned for me to follow him to the cabin. I was shaking so hard that I could hardly make my feet move. When we reached the cabin I began to babble some kind of thanks to him, but he just nodded and left.

We burst through the cabin door just as Mother was bursting out, only to be greeted by the smell of hot, wet dog. Laddie was curled up in front of the fire, Mittens between his paws as usual.

"He turned up right after you left," Mother said. "And I have been beside myself with worry about you. What was that shot?"

It took me a long time to calm her down.

When Father returned and Mother told him what

had happened, late though it was, he took off immediately with a sack of flour and a big pouch of his tobacco for John. He didn't come back until well after dark.

"It was little enough I could do to thank him," he said.

My hand is still trembling so that I can hardly read what I have written. But I am happy. Jamie refused to come up to the loft to sleep. I just peeked down and saw him curled up beside Laddie on the hearth. While I was watching, Grannie crept over and tucked a quilt around them both.

January 1st, 1785

We have had a lovely Hogmanay and it is still going on. Grannie and Mother and I had our cabin cleaned and scrubbed until it positively shone. Grannie made her wonderful oatcakes, sweetened with maple sugar that the Indians gave us, instead of the usual honey. They were delicious. No singing at the doors of neighbours' houses, of course, as the Rosses are half a day's journey away. But we celebrated anyway. Angus came in for supper and brought bannock that he had made. Who would ever have suspected he could do that?

Duncan did not appear and at first I was upset

about that, I must admit, but then I began to have a sneaking suspicion. Much to my delight my suspicion proved correct when there came a knock at the door just when it must have been around midnight. It was Duncan, playing the part of the first-foot. He brought bread that he had baked himself and a scuttle of burning coals to add to our fire. Warmth and comfort for the whole year, exactly what the first-foot is supposed to bring.

And then, today, a ringing of horses' bells and a great shouting brought us all outside just as we were about to sit down for dinner, and there was the whole Ross family with their horse and cart. What merriment! Jamie, George and Hugh took up right from where they had last left off, making mischief, and Molly was scolding as usual, but with sidelong glances at Angus all the while. Mother and Aunt Norah hugged each other and could not stop laughing and talking. Aunt Norah even hugged Grannie and Grannie almost hugged her back before she caught herself and remembered her dignity. Father and Uncle Andrew escaped all the noise and bustle as soon as they could and went outside to smoke their pipes, but Angus and Duncan stayed until it was time for them to go back to their own shanties.

Hannah and I have not stopped talking since she arrived. She is tucked up in bed with me now and I have just begged a few moments to bring my journal up to date and then we will start talking again. The boys are supposed to be asleep, but there are a lot of thumps and giggles coming from their side of the loft. I'm pretending not to notice it, but between the lot of them they have managed to smuggle Laddie up and he is under their quilts with them. I may not see him, but there's no mistaking the smell.

For the first time Hannah has admitted that maybe, just maybe, she fancies Alex Calder as much as he fancies her. For my part, I showed her the quilt I have begun to make.

"For my marriage," I said. "Although it will most certainly be a long way off."

"A long way off," she replied, "but I warrant I know who it will be to. Someone who seemed mighty proud of his socks, perhaps?"

Fortunately it was so dark that she couldn't see me blush. But it is all right for Hannah to know my secret. She is my best friend and always will be.

I am sitting here with a quilt around my shoulders. I can smell the wood smoke from our fire. The wind is just whispering around our walls tonight and it is warm and cosy in here. My candle is making dancing shadows on the walls and the boys have fallen silent at last. I hear a faint snoring but I think it is Laddie. Downstairs, Mother and Father are still talking quietly with Aunt Norah and Uncle Andrew. Molly must be fast asleep beside Grannie. I wonder if she is dreaming of Angus?

I remember last year around this time, thinking that home was a very sad word. That I would never have a home again. But you know what, dear journal of mine?

I was wrong.

Now Hannah is nudging me to put my journal away and get back to our talk.

So I will.

Harriet Palmer

A Trail of Broken Dreams

The Gold Rush Diary of Harriet Palmer
Overland to the Cariboo
May 1862 – October 1862

BY BARBARA HAWORTH-ATTARD

In 1862 Harriet Palmer undertook a treacherous overland journey from Manitoba to the Cariboo gold fields of British Columbia. On the journey she became close friends with Talbot Dyer and the Morgan brothers.

A Night to Rejoice

Tuesday, October 27, 1863

As gloomy a day as I've ever seen. Fog and drizzle roll into Victoria and the damp settles in the convent's brick walls, where it will stay all winter. But the weather suits my own dreary mood. I am writing this during Literature class. I just took a peek, and Sister does not seem to notice my inattention. The cause of my gloominess is that Talbot has not yet returned from the gold mines in the Cariboo. Joe and Henry Morgan arrived two weeks ago, Henry leaving immediately for business in San Francisco, Joe staying in Victoria. Talbot was to finish repairs to the water wheel at the gold claim on Williams Creek, and then winter here in Victoria. He *promised* me he'd see me at Christmas!

Tilly just poked me in the back. I best pay attention. Drawing is next — my favourite subject here at St. Ann's School. I have begun a portrait of Talbot, which I want to give to him at Christmas. (My most hated class is dancing. It appears my feet have a mind of their own.)

Thursday, November 26, 1863

I write this upon the deck of the steamer that takes Tilly, Joe and me to New Westminster. I am accompanying Tilly, who is heading home to a month of Christmas festivities, dances and parties with her betrothed, a man who she says lacks hair on his head, smells of damp and old age, and has hands that feel like wet fish. Her father has arranged the marriage. Tilly insisted I come with her, despite the three-year difference in our age, as she says I am the only person of sense she knows. That and the fact we are both without mothers created a bond between us when we first met at St. Ann's.

I jumped at the invitation because it meant I could ask after Talbot. He still has not arrived in Victoria, and will have to pass through New Westminster on his way from the Cariboo. Joe is accompanying us, and is quite puffed out with importance to be responsible for two young ladies. (Which is funny, since Henry asked me to keep an eye on his brother.)

It is a good sail today through the rocky, heavily treed islands. I would enjoy it except for Talbot's absence. Half the time I am vexed with him, half the time worried. Joe is concerned, too. Remembering all the troubles we faced on our trek from Fort Garry to the Cariboo last year assures me that Talbot can take care of himself. But we still hear stories of people freezing to death in the Cariboo during a fall blizzard, or injuries at the mines, or miners being hit over the head by a gold robber, or even murdered.

Monday, November 30, 1863

New Westminster

Mr. Miller, Tilly's betrothed, is not nearly as old as she says, though she is right that his hair is thinning and his hands do sweat profusely. I think it is because he is terrified of Tilly. She is quite beautiful and quite outspoken.

Joe and I spent yesterday wandering about town asking after Talbot. Joe wouldn't let me go into the taverns to ask the miners if they knew Talbot, which I found funny, given that I used to work in one in Richfield (though I suppose that doesn't quite count, since I was dressed as a boy). I did find it difficult to wait outside while Joe enquired within, but then I've always been too impatient.

No news of Talbot. My mind is now in a burning turmoil!

Tuesday, December 1, 1863

I have a plan.

Thursday, December 3, 1863

I am writing this by candlelight in the bush, so it is not my best penmanship. It took a day of talking and arguing to convince Joe to follow my plan, which was for us to travel to the Cariboo to find Talbot. I feel bad taking advantage of Joe's good nature. Henry would never have allowed us to travel all the way to the Cariboo in winter. He'd say it's far too dangerous to be trying to make our way to Barkerville. But I survived swamps and mountains and floods and hunger last year. In the end, I promised Joe we would turn back if it becomes too dangerous.

Tilly is with us also. She heard Joe and me whispering together, and knowing my worry about Talbot, guessed at my plan to go to the Cariboo to find him. She arrived in my room this evening with two sets of her father's clothes. At first I told her she couldn't come with us, but she said, "It is my last chance to have an adventure before I am married." I will admit I am glad of her company. We left a note for her father with one of the maids, with instructions that it not be given to him before noon tomorrow.

Tilly had great fun dressing up in her father's clothes and told me to call her Matt — never, ever Matilda. She hates her name. She already calls me Harry, so that shouldn't be a problem.

I had thought to go as a girl, but realized that pants will give us greater freedom of movement than long skirts trailing in snow, and the coats are bulky enough to hide our figures.

We slipped out late this evening after the house was quiet. As it is too late in the year for the steamers to run up the Fraser River, Joe hired two canoes and four Indians to take us to Langley. The first night we went only a little way from New Westminster, as we feared hitting rocks in the river in the dark. We are now camped along the shore. Joe has given us a good fire, and piled pine boughs for our beds. There is only a dusting of snow here and the river is clear of ice.

Friday, December 4, 1863

Langley

We are in Langley. It is early afternoon and raining. I am happy it is not snow. Two of our guides do not wish to go any farther, so Joe has gone to a lodge across the river to hire two others. While we wait, Tilly is practising swaggering about in her men's clothes. She even spat once, which brought on a fit of giggles for the two of us. What if her betrothed saw her now!

Later

Joe has returned. As dark comes so early, we will overnight here in a boarding house.

Monday, December 7, 1863

Fort Yale

Three full days of travel by canoe have us at Fort Yale this evening. We are staying at the Hudson's Bay Company House, with a friend of Henry and Joe's. We are glad for the warm fire. Joe had made the canoe comfortable with hay and blankets, but the rain changed to cold and snow, and even Tilly's high spirits are dampened.

The river was very low, so the guides had to do a great deal of poling, which was time consuming. Yesterday at Fort Hope we overnighted on the floor of a tavern. The town was full of miners. Joe told them the story I'd cooked up that Tilly and I were brothers trying to get to Barkerville, where our eldest brother was missing.

None of them had news of Talbot, though. Joe is teaching Tilly all the miners' sayings, such as "You bet your gumboots" and "your bottom dollar."

Wednesday, December 9, 1863

Boston Bar

Snow storming all day. Tired and exhausted. We secured passage yesterday in a trader's four-horse sleigh that was travelling to Boston Bar with freight. Well-wrapped in buffalo robes and blankets, we thought we would make good time along the Cariboo Wagon Road, but the snow wasn't very deep and we had to get in and out of the sleigh to ease the horses' load on the bare patches. Even despite this, one of the horses went lame!

We spent the night at the house of a farmer. Tilly and I helped the woman of the house with the dinner preparations, forgetting we were supposed to be boys. She seemed quite surprised until we told her we were quite used to getting dinner, as our mother was dead. The woman stared at Tilly all the evening long, making Tilly most uncomfortable. We did not talk other than to answer "yes" or "no." We will not stay in individual homes after this, as it gives people too much opportunity to discover that we are girls.

Finally made Boston Bar early this evening after another dreadful day of travel.

Thursday, December 10, 1863

We left at five in the morning in the dark and cold. The trader had agreed to Joe's request (and ten extra dollars!) to take us on to Lytton, and northwards to the ferry, which is as far as he will go. We reached the ferry late in the afternoon. The snow is deeper here, so the sleigh ran much better. Tilly is much impressed with the mountains, though less impressed with the narrow road cut into the sides of these mountains.

The ferry owner told us that there is snow, mud and mire ahead of us. He strongly advised us to turn back. Joe is worried, but I told him we should at least see the conditions for ourselves, as people tend to exaggerate.

Friday, December 11, 1863

We got such a shock this morning. As we were sitting down to a breakfast of beans and pancakes in our wayhouse, a loud voice said, "Matilda." Tilly's mouth dropped open and she turned quite pink. It was Mr. Miller! Many heads turned to watch with interest as he hauled Joe out of his chair and drew back an arm to hit him, but Tilly grabbed Mr. Miller and told him to stop. She pushed him into a room and slammed the door. Joe was very upset, but I told him to sit and eat his pancakes, as there was little sense in them going to waste, and I knew Tilly would smooth everything over.

Twenty minutes later, Tilly and Mr. Miller returned. Both looked quite pleased with themselves. Tilly sat down to her breakfast and said, "Mr. Miller will be accompanying us to the Cariboo." Mr. Miller hmphed and hawed a great deal, but finally sat with us. "And, Harry, I want to ask that you stand with me as my witness at our wedding, which will take place immediately upon our return to New Westminster."

I don't think Mr. Miller is all that old, now that I have seen him very close up. It is just that he has the misfortune of his hair thinning early.

Sunday, December 13, 1863

47-Mile House

We are at 47-Mile House. (Some people call it Clinton.) We travelled partway in a waggonnette, until the snow became too deep, then by horse and mule — Tilly and myself riding the mules! Never have I been so jolted about. Tilly whispered to me in our room, later, that her "arse" was sore. We giggled a long time over that.

A funny thing happened on the way. It was snowing fast and suddenly Tilly's mule shied and pranced about, and out of the curtain of white came a camel! Tilly's mouth fell open and I felt quite glad, because I *knew* she never believed me when I told her that I had been up on a camel's back when I came to the Cariboo. Mr. Miller was as surprised as Tilly. Joe told him that the camels had been brought to the Cariboo to be used as pack animals, but were not suited for the job. Where this one came from, I don't know, but it wandered away shortly after. The mules settled down after it left — they hate the smell of camels.

We are having a day of rest in Clinton, as the hotel is a good size and comfortable. Mr. Miller is feeling a bit seedy. A cold in his head. I asked Tilly if she was happy to be marrying him. She shrugged and said, "I must marry someone and it is all arranged." I pointed out to her that he came all this way after her. (It is my secret belief that Tilly has some affection for Mr. Miller.)

She thought about that for a moment, then turned the conversation to me by asking, "And what about you coming after Talbot? Do you care for him?" I made an excuse to leave the room as I didn't have an answer. I can tell *you*, dear diary, that I do care for Talbot, but whether as more than a friend, I am not sure.

Monday, December 14, 1863

I am most impatient to leave. Mr. Miller is still under the weather. I told Tilly to dose him with brandy. The longer we stay here, the worse the weather will be farther along. I am not sure I want him to come with us, as he is a bit of a dandy and I doubt he will cope well in the bush.

Evening

I am so glad we didn't leave. Perhaps patience is a virtue after all, as late this morning we had news of Talbot. Two miners arrived on their way to winter in New Westminster. They had left Williams Creek two weeks previous and spent some time in Barkerville before arriving here. (Drinking the town dry by the looks and smell of them, Tilly said.) They reported that early in November they had spoken to a young man named Talbot who was waiting for supplies to fix a water wheel. He told the miners that he would leave as soon as the supplies arrived, as he planned to spend Christmas with friends in Victoria! That's *me!* Or rather, Henry, Joe and me! But where is he? Mr. Miller wants to head back. He says that perhaps we passed each other en route and Talbot is already in New Westminster. But my gut (an unladylike word, I know, but Joe and I believe what our "gut" tells us) says Talbot is still on Williams Creek, so we're continuing. The sky was clear and the air cold, but we made good time and got to Lac la Hache. The scenery here is beautiful, evergreens darkening the lower slopes of the mountains, and the lake shimmering blue. My fingers itch to sketch it!

Mr. Miller knew of a Mr. Bates who had a ranch here. We were forced to stay the night, as there were not any inns or wayhouses nearby. Tilly constantly reminds Mr. Miller to call her Matt and me Harry. He called me Miss Palmer, but sneezed while doing so — I don't believe Mr. Bates heard him. Tilly and I retired early so we didn't have to talk.

Tuesday, December 15, 1863

Up before dawn. A bright, cold day. Mr. Bates will take us to Soda Creek to "try his new sleigh," he said.

Tuesday late

We only had one moment of concern this entire day, when one of the horses shied at the cry of a wild animal and the reins got all askew. We greatly admired Mr. Bates's new sleigh. He was so delighted with our praise, he decided to take us on to Quesnel Mouth tomorrow. There are many miners here, drinking and gambling. Mr. Miller, Mr. Bates and Joe have joined a game. I worry that Joe will lose everything.

Wednesday, December 16, 1863

150-Mile House

Tilly is hurt! I should never have let her come. It was snowing fast when we left Soda Creek at first light. We had passed 150-Mile House, when suddenly one of the horses floundered in a snowdrift and the sleigh plunged down a bank. Joe, Mr. Miller and I were flung clear, but Tilly and Mr. Bates went over the fifteen-foot drop. Thank goodness the thick snow cushioned their fall. Tilly's right ankle is twisted and her arm is sore from being tangled in the reins. Mr. Bates had a gash in his head, but otherwise appeared fine.

Mr. Miller showed some spunk and plunged down the hill with no thought for his own safety to rescue Tilly. She was quite impressed. The horses appear none the worse for the fall, but Tilly can go no farther.

Mr. Miller wanted us all to return to Soda Creek, saying Joe and I could not go on alone. But as you know, dear diary, I am very stubborn. Joe and I returned to 150-Mile House and managed to get two sickly mules that were left to winter there by miners. Fifteen dollars each, enough to buy 150 pounds of bacon! Presently we are camped by the trail, cold and hungry.

Friday, December 18, 1863

Quesnel Mouth

We arrived at Quesnel Mouth late yesterday. We had a frightening trip in a dugout canoe crossing the river to get here. Many times I thought we'd be swamped.

New stores have been built since the last time Joe and I stayed. Went farther north to a roadhouse owned by one of the overlanders who came with us last year. From here we'll go on foot to Cottonwood. No one here has seen or heard of Talbot. I'm not sure what to think.

Saturday, December 19, 1863, late

We slept late and then were delayed, as I insisted on questioning more people for news of Talbot. Mr. Miller had put the doubt in my mind that even now Talbot might be in Victoria (despite what my gut says).

Slow progress on foot — I had forgotten the weight of a pack on one's back! My shoulders are rubbed raw. Joe and I traded our boots for comfortable miners' gumboots that had been cast away at the side of the trail. The ones I found were too large and I stuffed them with cloth; Joe found a pair that fit him well. It took us a long time to wade through snowdrifts and in some places knee-deep mud. We made little progress and are camped in the bush, not wanting to venture farther in the dark. Dead horses and mules line the trail, starved from lack of food. Thank goodness for the cold weather, or the stink of them . . .

Later still!

I must continue, though I do so with one eye on my book and one on the strange man across the fire from me. We heard crashing in the woods and suddenly a man staggered to our fire. Joe grabbed his revolver!

The man's clothes were in tatters, his hat just a rim and his shirt shredded. There were no pants below his knees. His eyes were wild. He asked if he could share our fire. We asked him what had happened, and he said that he'd been set upon by thieves who left him nothing. We didn't feel right turning him away, but I saw Joe lie down with his revolver by his head.

Monday, December 21, 1863, noon

Past Cottonwood

We made little progress yesterday. We both were exhausted from keeping an eye on the strange man, though we must have slept at some point, as he was gone come morning.

My legs cramped because they are unused to the hard walking. My feet are blistered. Dreadful night. Slept on the floor in a wayside house just outside of Cottonwood. Only one blanket apiece and wind howling through the cracks in the walls and floor.

Monday evening

Richfield

We are in the French Hotel in Richfield. I'm a girl again — or rather, people here remember me as a girl. In the bar there are three women in male attire playing cards! They are even smoking cigars. Joe said I wasn't to mix with them.

No news of Talbot. Snow flies thick and fast. I want to go to Williams Creek tomorrow, but Joe has been told it would be foolhardy and we would never make it. I can't be *this* close, dear diary, and not at least try to get to the gold claim. I think of Talbot out there alone in the dark and cold.

Tuesday, December 22, 1863

Snowing still. Even I can see the danger of travelling. Tomorrow I will go no matter what the weather. I won't tell Joe, as I'd feel bad if he was hurt or killed. I'll go to bed like normal tonight, then leave at first light before anyone is up.

Wednesday, December 23, 1863

Snowed in. I despair of ever finding Talbot.

Thursday, December 24, 1863, night

Barkerville

I found Talbot! He is quite ill with a broken leg, boils and a fever, but Dr. Black says he should mend soon.

I will now record how it came about that we discovered him. I got up early yesterday, as planned, and nearly tripped over Joe, who was sleeping outside my door — guarding me, he said, but I think he knows me too well. The snow had stopped and though the sky was steel grey with the promise of more to come, we walked to Barkerville. There we had a hot drink, then continued to Williams Creek. A light snow drifted down, but more troublesome was a dense fog that formed. Joe had been that way many times, though, and we stayed close to the creek to guide our way. We came across a few men wintering on their claims, and warmed up in the cabin of one. None had seen Talbot.

My heart beat fiercely as we approached the claim, my imagination running wild with all sorts of horrors. The cabin door was closed, a drift of snow in front of it to the roof. Joe cleared it away and inside we found Talbot! I nearly cried to see him so thin and sick and trembling, and in fact, turned to the task of building the fire so he wouldn't see my tears. He was out of his mind and thought Joe and I weren't real, until I took his cold hand and pressed it hard so he'd know it really was us, flesh and bone.

Joe made a sleigh and we strapped Talbot to it and pulled him to Barkerville, where Dr. Black took him in. I saw Talbot for a few minutes this evening and he is washed and clean and sleepy. He told me he waited until mid-November for the water-wheel engine to come, and then slipped on an icy patch while fixing it, and fell and broke his leg. He managed to drag in some wood for heat, and tried to set his leg himself, but it wouldn't heal and he got weaker and weaker and the past week had neither heat nor food. He told me he thought he was "done for."

We will stay here in Barkerville until Talbot is better. Once again, I am at the mercy of Mrs. McManus, where I will stay until we can travel. A packer is planning to make his way to New Westminster later this week, so agreed to take a letter to Tilly. I asked her to send one on to Victoria for me. I imagine I will be missed at school, and surprisingly, for all the wandering that my feet insist upon, I'll miss it. For now though, I am very happy. Talbot kept his promise that we'd be together for Christmas, though I thought it would be in Victoria, not Barkerville!

But it does not matter where we are; it is Christmas Eve, and Talbot is safe. It truly is a night to rejoice.

Susanna Merritt

Whispers of War

The War of 1812 Diary of Susanna Merritt
Niagara, Upper Canada

May 1812 – November 1812

BY KIT PEARSON

Susanna Merritt and her family have had a difficult year as the fighting between British and American troops intensified — fighting that has involved Susanna's father and her brother Hamilton. The work of running the farm has fallen to Susanna, her sister Maria and her mother. Caroline, her married sister, is staying with them while her husband is away with the troops. Susanna, as is her habit, writes in her journal as if she is talking to her future great-granddaughter, Constance.

No Room for Christmas

11 December 1813

Dear Constance,

My hand shakes as I record the worst disaster of this terrible year: The Americans have burnt Niagara completely to the ground! That awful General McClure decided to pull his troops back to the United States, but before they left he gave the order to torch Niagara. The townspeople had only half an hour to leave their houses. All four hundred of them had to stand in the bitter cold in the middle of the night, watching their homes be consumed in flames.

One was old Hannah. She stood in front of Papa's Niagara house, guarding the few possessions she was able to get outside by herself. Papa took a sleigh from the British headquarters at Burlington Heights and brought Hannah back here. Then he had to leave for Burlington again.

Hannah has been sitting with us in the parlour all

afternoon. She is not hurt from the fire. I have never been fond of her (as you well know, Constance), but she has been a loyal housekeeper to Papa for many years. She told us she made a spirited protest to the Americans when they put the first torch to Papa's house, shouting at them that they would pay for their wickedness. "They might have harmed you!" said Maria, but I admire Hannah's courage.

Hannah will now live with us and help Tabitha with the cooking and housework. She will have to share Tabitha's small room off the kitchen. Tabitha is not happy about that, but where else are we to put a second servant?

This house is already too full. How many more people can it hold until it bursts?

12 December 1813

Dear Constance,

Hamilton was here for supper. He told me how all of Niagara, that beloved place that gave us so much pleasure, has been reduced to heaps of smouldering coals. Then he said something shocking, that he is glad that Niagara was burnt, for it means the Americans are losing.

"How can you say that, when so much harm was done?" I asked him. Hamilton said he was sorry that the town was destroyed, but such things happen in war. "McClure is a coward," he said angrily. "We must do something to retaliate."

I am so sad that my brother feels this way. At the beginning of this war he did not want to fight, and now his whole life is fighting. I know he goes on dangerous raids, but he does not talk about them.

The house is full of ill feelings. Hannah told Mama that she cannot share a bed with Tabitha because Tabitha snores. She wants Tabitha's room to herself. Mama does not dare cross her — Hannah is so fierce, she frightens all of us. So my poor Tabitha has to sleep on a mattress in a corner of the kitchen. I tried to make it as comfortable as possible for her, and offered her Mouse as a companion. She thanked me, but muttered angrily about "that interloper." There are no kind words between the two of them, and the atmosphere in the kitchen is so icy I hate to go in there.

Little Adelaide is cutting a new tooth. All afternoon I had to mind her while Caroline and the others were plucking the ducks Hamilton shot. When Adelaide was an infant I greatly enjoyed looking after her. Now she is — I cannot help saying — a most unpleasant, whiny child.

Adelaide screamed for her mother and would not be soothed. Finally Tabitha dipped a cloth in brandy and gave it to her to suck. She fell asleep in my arms and I put her in her cot.

The others are all chatting downstairs but I am in my room. Adelaide is breathing peacefully. I am afraid to go to bed until Maria and Caroline come up. Last night I had terrible nightmares about Niagara burning. The flames have been in my head all day. I keep remembering all the rooms of Papa's beautiful house, especially the bedroom where Maria and I slept when we were in town. I kept an old doll there, one Mama made for me on my fifth birthday. Her name was Rebecca. I am far too old for dolls now, of course, but it breaks my heart to think of Rebecca being consumed by fire.

I am so lonesome. Even though the Americans have left the fort, there are still numerous raids. It is too dangerous to leave the farm, so I am not allowed to visit Abbie or Elias. How I long to speak to someone my own age!

Soon Christmas will be here, but no one has said a word about it. Last year we were gathering evergreen boughs and Tabitha was making plum pudding. Maria and I were hiding our presents from each other.

But last year there was a lull in the fighting. This year the war permeates every corner of our lives. There is no room for Christmas.

16 December 1813

Dear Constance,

Caroline told Mama that I have been cruel to Adelaide. I have not! All I did was shake her a little when she was demanding to have another piece of duck pie. I am so tired of Adelaide. I am tired of humouring her, of changing her smelly diaper, of wiping her runny nose.

Mama took me into her room and asked me to pray with her to be more generous toward Adelaide. I tried to pray, but I know God was not listening. He is too busy with the war. Mama also asked me to try to understand that it is hard for Caroline to be crammed into our house rather than being at her own, with James there to make them all a family.

Tabitha and Hannah are still at odds. Tabitha told me that Hannah is lazy. She spends most of her time crocheting in front of the fire. I tried to tell Tabitha that Hannah is old, and reminded her that Hannah has served our family for many years, but Tabitha retorted that she is healthy and strong and should be helping more.

It is bitterly cold. This morning the water in the washstand basin was frozen, and I had to shroud my face in my shawl when I collected the eggs. Every night I heat up a stone and wrap it in a blanket to warm our bed. It does not help much. I squeeze against plump Maria to try to get warm and she pushes me away, saying I am poking her.

Dear Constance,

It is still very cold. This morning I helped Mama bring in the frozen clothes, which had been outside to dry. I asked her if we were going to celebrate Christmas this year. She looked at me wearily. "I am sorry, my dear child, but I cannot promise you much for Christmas. We have no time to spare for it and we do not even know if your father and brother will be here." She smiled, and told me that we would try to say some special prayers and sing some carols. My heart grew heavy and I did not dare to mention greenery or baking or presents.

Last year, as in all the other years of my life, we went to church on Christmas morning. The bells rang and we sang lustily and all the people greeted each other so warmly afterwards. But we have not had any church services at all this year, and we never see our neighbours. I fear that Abbie will hardly know me by the time we're allowed to visit again.

Tonight I asked Maria if she would play some carols on the piano. She said she was too busy sewing

Charles a shirt. I tried to pick out the tune to "While Shepherds Watched Their Flocks By Night," but it sounded like a dirge.

22 December 1813

Dear Constance,

Once more the war suffocates us. There has been another battle, and the house is full of strangers.

Here is what happened: on December 18, Fort Niagara was taken by our Colonel Murray in retaliation for the Americans' burning of Niagara. Then Lewiston was attacked. And then every house on the American side of the river, from Fort Niagara to Tonawanda Creek, was burned! Although this was a great gain for our side, I find it horrifying that so much destruction was necessary.

Here is the reason for the strangers: Papa arrived with an *American* family! They are the Leonards, the wife and children of Captain Leonard, who is now in prison. They were stationed with him at Fort Niagara. Mama was overjoyed to see them — she knew the Leonards years ago in South Carolina.

Their arrival causes me once more to reflect on how absurd this war is. The Leonards are officially our enemy. Yet Mama and Papa themselves used to be Americans! I am glad that Papa had the generosity to rescue Mama's old friend, in spite of the fact that he is fighting against her husband.

There are two girls, Miss Leonard and her younger sister, Miss Phoebe Leonard. Miss Leonard is reserved and haughty. Phoebe is a year younger than me. She is plain looking, with a scrawny neck and thin light hair.

Mrs. Leonard and Miss Leonard are sleeping in Mama's room. Phoebe is on a cot in ours. So there are now five of us crammed in here.

Mama has told me I must be especially hospitable to Phoebe. I have tried to talk to her, but she puts down her head and does not answer. It is difficult to communicate with someone who does not wish to be friends.

Poor Phoebe must be worrying about her father constantly, so I cannot blame her for not responding. How distraught I would be if Papa or Hamilton or James or Charles were imprisoned!

Later

I invited Phoebe to come to the barn with me to feed the pigs, and she followed me silently. But then she finally spoke! She told me that she had had her own pig on her farm in New York. "When the war started we had to live in the fort," she said sadly.

I asked her if she had liked living there, and she said it was very tedious. "How I miss school and my friends!" she added.

"So do I!" I told her, and went on to talk about Abbie and Elias and how much I miss visiting them. Because it was so cold, we could not linger in the barn. Phoebe helped me carry the eggs to the pantry and we continued our conversation there.

Our words tumbled over each other's. We have so much in common! We are both fond of animals, reading and writing. Phoebe keeps a diary, as well!

Phoebe said shyly, "I do not know how long we will be staying here, Susanna, but I would be honoured to be your friend."

I smiled so hugely that I thought my face might crack.

23 December 1813

Dear Constance,

Last night Maria generously gave up her half of the bed to Phoebe and slept on Phoebe's cot. This enabled us to whisper and giggle for a long time, until my sisters insisted that we be quiet.

This morning I woke up with such a light heart I had trouble remembering what has changed: I have a new friend! Phoebe and I did all my chores together, which greatly speeded them up. She is much more patient with Adelaide than I.

After dinner we sat in a corner of the parlour with our sewing, while our mothers chattered about people they used to know. That was when we made our plan.

When Papa was here he shot us a brace of geese, so at least we will have a Christmas feast. We do not know if the men can be here for it, but they will try to be. Mama says that is all we will have: a good dinner, some prayers, and some carols in the parlour.

There is no time to make presents, but Phoebe's and my idea will be a present for everyone.

24 December 1813

Dear Constance,

This morning Mama let me take Phoebe for a ride around the farm in the cutter. The air was cold, but we were well bundled in furs and I wore my new rabbit-skin mittens. The sky was an intense blue, and the bare trees looked black against it. The snow sparkled like jewels. I was proud of how beautiful Queen looked, tossing her head and prancing.

Phoebe was overjoyed to be in a sleigh again. We went over every detail of our surprise for tomorrow, then sang "The Boar's Head" at the top of our voices.

When we got home, Phoebe and I gathered spruce

boughs and wintergreen to decorate the house. We hung them all over the parlour and dining room and they look so festive. The prettiest is the kissing-bough we made out of twigs, greenery and apples, which we hung from the ceiling in the parlour. It is as if the house is saying, "I do not care if there is a war, I am going to celebrate Christmas anyway."

I am so excited about tomorrow that I doubt I will sleep. I did not think that Maria or Phoebe's sister would be interested in our plan, but they caught us preparing for it in our room, so we told them. Now they are going to take part! I cannot believe that Miss Leonard would want to help, but she is the most avid of us all. She even said that I could call her Jemima.

Tomorrow is the birth date of the Saviour. The night is clear and cold, and there are many stars gleaming in the black sky. Everyone else is asleep, but I am sitting by the window with my small flame. It strikes me that people have celebrated this birth for centuries and that you, Constance, will still be celebrating it in the future. This is a hopeful thought, a light in the darkness of this year of war. I have not felt so uplifted for a long, long time. And now I will try to sleep.

25 December 1813

Dear Constance,

This has been the best Christmas I have ever had. A few months ago I would never have believed that. All the Christmases I remember have been joyful, but they have also been much the same. This one was special because I — and Phoebe and Maria and Jemima and even little Adelaide — made it happen.

Even though it is now very late, I have to write down every detail before I blow out my candle. I woke up early, to a bright, sparkly morning. I gathered the eggs and helped Tabitha put the bread into the oven. Hannah slept late, but when she came out she was in a good mood for once, and wished me a happy Christmas.

I did not think there would be any presents this year, but how wrong I was! The first was from Tabitha, an ivory needle case that used to belong to her mother. I will always treasure it. Then Hannah presented me with a shawl! She had also made one for Tabitha. "I am sorry I have not been very friendly, Miss Holland," she said gruffly. "Shall we try to get on better next year? I would be glad if you would move back into your room again." Tabitha smiled and said that the two of them could share it. I stood gaping at this first miracle of the day.

Everyone came down for breakfast and exchanged Christmas kisses. Tabitha had made flapjacks — I had three and Phoebe five! We kept glancing at each other, almost bursting with our secret.

Then *all* the men arrived! Papa and Hamilton and James and Charles. James tossed Adelaide into the air until she shrieked with joy. All day she has been good; perhaps she was naughty before because she missed her father.

Maria was beside herself with bliss — she had thought that Charles would spend Christmas with his sister. She took him off to the parlour and Mama forgot to send me in as a chaperone. Perhaps they were sitting under the kissing-bough!

Papa and Hamilton hugged me and I sat on Papa's knee, even though I am far too big to do so. He slipped an English shilling into my pocket as my Christmas present.

Then I noticed how sad Phoebe looked — she and Jemima were missing their father terribly, of course. Papa assured them that he would be well taken care of. "Perhaps the war will over next year and he will be released," he said. Mrs. Leonard wept a little and Mama comforted her.

We went into the parlour, where we caught Maria and Charles with very red faces! In a stuttering voice Charles asked Papa for Maria's hand in marriage.

Papa laughed and gave his permission, saying that he was not at all surprised. Mama hugged Maria and wept.

Then Papa read us the Christmas lesson from the prayer book. He prayed for our safety and the end of this terrible war. I fervently added my own silent prayers. Today I felt for certain that God was listening.

We spent the rest of the morning and early afternoon preparing for our large Christmas feast. While I was shelling walnuts, Hamilton came into the kitchen and gave me the same present he gives me every year, a brand-new journal! I was amazed he had been able to find me one, but he said he got it in York months ago.

During the morning it transpired that everyone had been secretly planning presents for each other! I received a comb from Mama, a thimble from Caroline and a beautiful red ribbon from Maria. Phoebe and I announced that our present was for everyone and would come later in the day.

What a delicious dinner we had! Roast goose stuffed with apples, smoked ham, pickled onions, warm bread and honey, and preserved peaches. Tabitha's present was a plum pudding she had made in secret. She doused it in brandy and carried it in flaming, while we all cheered.

After dinner I informed the adults that they had to stay in the kitchen for half an hour, while we prepared a surprise. Then we left for the parlour, taking Adelaide with us.

Finally, after much laughter and confusion, we were ready. I stepped into the kitchen, took a deep breath, and announced in my loudest voice that everyone was invited to come into the parlour to receive their present: a performance of the Christmas story.

They all cried with delight in a most gratifying way! Then they crowded into the parlour and stayed near one end to give us room.

At the other end we had curtained off a portion of the room for costume changes. I sat on a stool in front of the curtain with my script and began to read: "And it came to pass in those days, that there went out a decree from Caesar Augustus, that all the world should be taxed."

So began our play. First Phoebe and Jemima appeared, Phoebe draped in blue muslin and Jemima wearing Hamilton's coat. We had stuffed a pillow under Phoebe's dress. I hoped Caroline would not say that this was improper, but she seemed to join in the appreciation that everyone in the room was expressing.

Mary and Joseph travelled down the middle of the room and back, then sat in the corner we had lined with straw to be the stable. I had put Mouse there to be a stable cat and, miraculously, she stayed and curled up in the straw.

When I read that Jesus was born, Phoebe pulled out the pillow (the audience chuckled), Maria handed Adelaide out from behind the curtain, and Phoebe took her in her lap. This was my biggest worry: would Adelaide cry for her parents and leave the play? She began to whimper, but Phoebe gave her some comfits and Adelaide snuggled in Phoebe's lap, happily chewing. She looked as sweet and innocent as the real baby Jesus. I felt sorry that I have not been kinder to Adelaide and vowed to keep her happy for the rest of the war.

Jemima slipped behind the curtain and changed into tattered shepherd clothes. Maria appeared as the angel. How beautiful she looked in her white ball gown, with the wings we had fashioned of branches and goose feathers! Charles's face was radiant when he saw her. Maria's voice was so full of passion as she cried, "Fear not: for, behold, I bring you good tidings of great joy, which shall be to all people." All of us shouted, "Glory to God in the highest, and on earth peace, good will toward men." Tears came to my eyes as Hamilton's deep voice joined in.

We had to leave out the Wise Men, as there were not enough of us. Jemima changed back into Joseph and joined Mary and the Baby as I ended with the words: "But Mary kept all these things, and pondered them in her heart."

It was such a short play, yet it seemed to take years to perform. How everyone clapped and cheered! We all bowed and Adelaide crowed with delight. In that small room there was so much goodwill that I felt it could spread through the whole world.

After all the exclaiming and congratulations and thanks had settled down, Maria began playing carols while we gathered round to sing. We sang "Adeste Fideles," "Christians, Awake!" and "Lift Up Your Heads in Joyful Hope," just like other Christmases.

When it was very late, and we were sitting drowsily with brandy and walnuts, the men had to go back to Burlington. We tried not to weep as we kissed them goodnight, then kissed each other and went to bed.

I sit here now while my sisters, my niece, and my new friend are sleeping. Christmas Day is almost over.

Who knows what next year may bring? I pray for an end to the war. I pray that Papa and Hamilton and James and Charles will not be wounded or killed. I pray that Phoebe's father will soon be released.

Mostly I pray in gratitude that I am blessed with such a loving family and friends. No matter how bad the war becomes, we have each other.

"Glory to God in the highest, and on earth peace!"

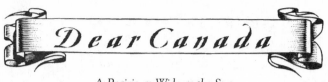

Dear Canada

A Prairie as Wide as the Sea
The Immigrant Diary of Ivy Weatherall
by Sarah Ellis

Orphan at My Door
The Home Child Diary of Victoria Cope
by Jean Little

With Nothing But Our Courage
The Loyalist Diary of Mary MacDonald
by Karleen Bradford

Footsteps in the Snow
The Red River Diary of Isobel Scott
by Carol Matas

A Ribbon of Shining Steel
The Railway Diary of Kate Cameron
by Julie Lawson

Whispers of War
The War of 1812 Diary of Susanna Merritt
by Kit Pearson

Alone in an Untamed Land
The Filles du Roi Diary of Hélène St. Onge
by Maxine Trottier

Brothers Far from Home
The World War I Diary of Eliza Bates
by Jean Little

An Ocean Apart
The Gold Mountain Diary of Chin Mei-ling
by Gillian Chan

Banished from Our Home
The Acadian Diary of Angélique Richard
by Sharon Stewart

A Trail of Broken Dreams
The Gold Rush Diary of Harriet Palmer
by Barbara Haworth-Attard

Winter of Peril
The Newfoundland Diary of Sophie Loveridge
by Jan Andrews

Turned Away
The World War II Diary of Devorah Bernstein
by Carol Matas

The Death of My Country
The Plains of Abraham Diary of Geneviève Aubuchon
by Maxine Trottier

No Safe Harbour
The Halifax Explosion Diary of Charlotte Blackburn
by Julie Lawson

A Rebel's Daughter
The 1837 Rebellion Diary of Arabella Stevenson
by Janet Lunn